SMART, BUT DEAD

An Aggie Mundeen Mystery

Nancy G. West

HENERY PRESS

SMART BUT DEAD
An Aggie Mundeen Mystery
Part of the Henery Press Mystery Collection

First Edition
Trade paperback edition | November 2015

Henery Press
www.henerypress.com

ISBN-13: 978-1-943390-25-0

Printed in the United States of America

Praise for the Aggie Mundeen Mystery Series

SMART, BUT DEAD (#3)

"Hurrah for Aggie Mundeen, an effervescent heroine who finds trouble wherever she goes even when the initial pursuit is purely intellectual. Aggie's pluck, humor, intelligence and loving heart will always keep her young and always make readers smile."

– Carolyn Hart,
Agatha Award-Winning Author of *Ghost to the Rescue*

"*Smart*. Aggie Mundeen is smart. *But*. But she's also a little clumsy, irrepressible, and irresistible. *Dead*. She might well end up dead if she continues nosing around the university where her questions are not wanted. *Smart, But Dead* is the perfect combination of brains and heart. A tight mystery, an irrepressible heroine, and superb writing."

– James W. Ziskin,
Anthony Award-Nominated Author of *No Stone Unturned*

"*Smart, But Dead* features an impetuous, warm-hearted heroine, blessed with an insatiable curiosity, passion for learning and an unquenchable zest for life."

– *Mystery People*

"Will keep you guessing until the last page. Very well-written and excellent storyline. Highly recommended!"

– *Obsessed Book Reviews*

DANG NEAR DEAD (#2)

"Well-paced and written, there are bursts of humour in this novel which had me roaring with laughter. The plot is intricate, with a satisfying ending...A great read and highly recommended."

– Diana Hockley,
Australian Mystery Novelist

"A satisfying mystery with complex characters and a plot that builds to a satisfying crescendo."

– Midwest Book Review

"Suspenseful, engaging, funny, and unique. I loved following Aggie as she asked questions and followed clues. You will fall in love with Nancy G. West's writing just as I have!"

– Universal Creativity Reviews

FIT TO BE DEAD (#1)

"*Fit to Be Dead* has it all: intriguing characters that point to romance, an engrossing plot, a compelling puzzle and well-disguised clues—a fun read."

– L. C. Hayden,
Award-Winning Author of the Harry Bronson Mystery Series

"West's main characters' histories suggest they could fill a series. I hope so. I love this book!"

– Rollo K. Newsom PhD,
Professor Emeritus, Texas State University,
and an editor of Lone Star Sleuths

"From the first sentence, readers receive a satisfying sense of West's fun plays on words: 'Shaping up at my age can be murder....I'm mechanically inept. My condition may be genetic.'"

– Midwest Book Review

"Aggie Mundeen's wry observations on life, death, and the struggle to whip mind and body into shape make *Fit to Be Dead* delightful. Joining a health club has never been so dangerous...or so amusing."

– Karen McCullough,
Author of Shadow of a Doubt and A Question of Fire

SMART,
BUT
DEAD

**The Aggie Mundeen Mystery Series
by Nancy G. West**

FIT TO BE DEAD (#1)
DANG NEAR DEAD (#2)
SMART BUT DEAD (#3)

ACKNOWLEDGMENTS

Without input from every person below, this book simply wouldn't exist. I am incredibly grateful for your knowledge, help and support.

- Sergeant Eva Adams
- Dr. Laura Cox
- Dr. Cynthia Kenyon
- Dr. Joseph Lambert
- Dr. Mary Lambert
- Dr. Doug P. Lyle
- Detective Raymond Roberts
- Attorney John Robertson
- Anthony V. Rodriguez
- Attorney Bucky Tennison
- Presiding County Magistrate Michael Ugarte
- Corporal Stephanie Vega
- Lieutenant Jesse Vera
- Dr. Donald West
- Dr. Luci Zahray
- The excellent editors at Henery Press

Any errors that exist in the novel are mine.

I do not, however, accept responsibility for whatever Aggie Mundeen might do.

One

At some point, the same thought hits everybody over thirty: *I might actually get old.* Since I was pushing forty, single, and attracted to a reluctant San Antonio detective, that nasty thought frequently wormed its way to the front of my brain.

I wrote the column "Stay Young with Aggie," answering readers' questions about how to stay youthful. For me, it was the ideal job, since my greatest fear was catapulting headlong into middle-age decrepitude.

So I made a decision: 1997 was the year I'd learn to avoid aging.

This was the perfect time to act. Scientists were in the middle of the Human Genome Project, a fifteen-year study to determine the location and function of every human gene. They'd already discovered genetic anomalies that caused disease, which was their main focus, but they'd also found genetic links to aging. Those tidbits propelled me back to college. Could scientists alter people's genes to keep them young?

Meredith Laughlin and I were driving to University of the Holy Trinity for fall semester to take the class Science of Aging. In Texas, in the third week of August, temperatures still hovered in the high nineties. The breath of fall wouldn't tickle San Antonio until mid-October. College kids didn't seem to notice, but my arms would be sticky five minutes after I left the air-conditioned car. Despite the heat, expectations about discovering genetic links to aging heightened my senses like cold gusts from a norther.

Scientists were making astounding genetic advancements. University of Edinburgh scientists had cloned a domestic female sheep from an adult mammary gland cell. Unable to think of a "more impressive pair of glands than Dolly Parton's," scientists named the sheep Dolly, and she had been alive and healthy for a year. With genetics unleashed—and scientists' humor alive and well—I had every reason to hope they'd soon be able to replace aging cells with young ones.

"Aren't you excited by the prospect of staying young?" I asked Meredith, my heart thumping like a metronome. I was further out of college than she was, about fifteen years further. Fear of aging oppressed me like humidity.

"I'm always eager when a new class starts," she said. When she hit a speed bump on the entry road to UHT, my stomach leaped into my throat. Studying had lifted me from tight spots in my life. Meredith was curious about the subject, but at age twenty-four, her need was less. For me, the course was mandatory.

We wheeled deeper into campus. Students emerged from parked cars, chatting excitedly as they walked toward the main building to check in.

I squinted up through the tree canopy that skirted brick buildings and inhaled fresh air from the cloudless Texas sky. The university clock tower rose skyward, a symbol of the timeless value of learning. A pinnacle of hope. A pointed reminder that a person couldn't wait forever.

Having concluded a silent prayer that my hopes would materialize, I blinked away sunspots and squinted down through branches at the administration building. I vowed to behave appropriately in class and not shoot off a barrage of challenging questions. Dr. Carmody might toss me from class or expel me from the university. He had nearly done it before. I had to contain myself.

My plan was to absorb the secrets of staying young from Dr. Carmody while I increased Detective Sam Vanderhoven's interest in me. My body was ticking like that clock.

As Meredith swung into a row of parked cars searching for a space, I craned behind her to get a better look at the man standing in front of the building fumbling with his briefcase. His bald eagle head had a fringe of light hair around the base. His shoulders weren't noticeably wide, but his body fanned out from there, ending in a triangle at his hips. A bald eagle head on a bear body? The man had to be Dr. Carmody. Maybe I could catch him before class and make peace.

"Meredith, stop," I said.

She hit the brake.

"Let me out. That's Carmody."

I sprinted toward him, motoring at full speed. He turned to ascend the steps to the building. With the sun blinding me, I plowed into his backside. I didn't particularly like him since he nearly booted me from his Aspects of Aging class, but I admired him, and I definitely didn't want to knock him down.

He spun back around, dropping his case. I bent to pick it up. When I rose and looked up, we were stomach to stomach. He grabbed my arm to steady himself. Once he stabilized, I stepped back and apologized.

"Dr. Carmody. I'm so sorry I crashed into you."

He jerked his head back to view me through his bifocals. "Oh. It's you."

Hairs protruding from his beak were grayer. Stiffer. His nose was the same size. Huge. He peered at me through frames heavy with Coke-bottle lenses heavily resting on his proboscis. I was surprised his glasses hadn't been recalled.

"You're that...that..."

"I'm Agatha Mundeen. Aggie, actually."

"I thought you'd left the university. You seemed reluctant to be in class. Somewhat hostile." He sniffed, peered over his lenses and tucked his chin into his neck. "Perhaps because of being outnumbered by, ahem, younger students?"

His remark irritated me, but I dared not let on. "No, not at all. I loved your class. I learned a lot."

He frowned as if trying to recall something unpleasant he'd just thought of, but he gave up.

I tried to bring him back to the moment. "I've been looking forward to your next class."

His gray unibrow shot up. "You're not..."

"I'm taking Science of Aging." I smiled. "I can hardly wait."

Color oozed up into his face. Blinking repeatedly, he planted his feet wider, securing balance, and gazed to far horizons. He finally squinted back at me.

I was face to face with the ultimate expert, but he appeared confused.

"You could stem the ravages of age," I said. "Not just for you and me but for everybody. I want to learn enough to write about some of your discoveries in my column. You could change the future for everyone on the planet. I want to be part of that."

The lines in his face softened. "I see. That's a lot to ask. I'll try to live up to your perception of what I can do."

"I know you will," I said. Taking a deep breath, I continued. "Dr. Carmody?"

"Yes?"

"I'm sorry I challenged you in your Aspects of Aging class. I get curious and feel so driven to learn quickly that sometimes I get overzealous."

"I understand." He smiled. "One has to be zealous to make discoveries. Actually, we've engaged in some new research. The results might be perfect for your column."

"That would be fantastic," I said with growing excitement. Had we come to some sort of understanding—even mutual respect?

He gazed up. His eyes took on a faraway look, as if he'd been transported to another realm.

I sighed. Our moment of camaraderie had taken flight.

He looked heavenward again and squeezed his eyes shut, as if trying to force something out from behind them. He finally opened his eyes and looked at me with a different expression.

"Well then, Anna...Amanda...Augusta..."

I knitted my brows together. Had he forgotten me already? He knew me well enough a second before. I stretched closer to his lenses. They were so smudged, maybe he couldn't see.

"It's Aggie. Aggie Mundeen."

He stared back. I waited. He blinked repeatedly and shook his head from side to side, as if fighting off a force I couldn't see.

"Well then," he said, "I'll see you in class." We smiled a truce.

He turned to gaze up at the edifice, put his briefcase in his left hand, grabbed the iron rail with his right and studied the building a long time before starting his ascent. Like a walrus lumbering from a pool.

Meredith walked up with our book bags. "What's the matter? You look ill."

I crumpled onto the step. "It's Dr. Carmody. Something's wrong with him. He recognized me, we discussed his research to delay aging, and he said something they're working on might be perfect for my column."

"That sounds wonderful."

"Yes. He knows more about how genes affect aging than anyone in the area. He directs the university research lab. Scientists come to consult him on the latest genetic discoveries. I *have* to learn about anti-aging from Dr. Carmody. I've waited months to take his class."

"Well, we're here."

"A few seconds after he said he might have something for my column, he forgot who I was. I wonder if he can even teach the class."

She checked her watch. "Let's go inside and find out."

Two

We entered the administration building. It was one of the oldest buildings at UHT, but it was cool inside—a gathering place for boisterous students.

Revived by air conditioning and slurping water from the fountain, I felt better. Maybe the heat had sapped poor Dr. Carmody. It happened to everybody in Texas sooner or later. I inhaled familiar odors of musty classrooms, new textbooks and perspiring students. University odors smelled better when you were eager to learn.

We trudged upstairs to Carmody's class on the second floor. The Registrar's Office probably assigned him a room close to the parking lot because of his out-of-shape condition. I felt sorry for him, having to routinely lumber up these stairs even in temperate weather.

We shuffled in and found seats. Carmody stood in front of the class and peered through smeared lenses at his groundlings, looking like his old imperious self. I relaxed. He announced he was Professor Kermit Carmody, Ph.D. and sniffed, causing his nose hairs to disappear. Temporarily. I should have selected a seat farther back.

He looked at the ceiling, took a deep breath and sighed before he started to lecture. "Welcome to Science of Aging. We're going to learn how genes affect certain diseases and may, we believe, affect the aging process."

A wide smile spread across my face. This was why I came.

"Since our class will be based on discoveries resulting from the Human Genome Project, the first step is understanding the genome," he said, pivoting toward me and squinting a warning to remain silent.

At least he recognized me. I sat straighter and forced down the corners of my mouth to appear serious and dedicated.

"The genome is the blueprint for an organism written in a code," Dr. Carmody continued. "This code is called deoxyribonucleic acid, DNA. To keep it simple, DNA is nothing more than a large molecule made up of four smaller molecules known by their initials: A, T, C, and G. These molecules always pair up: A always pairs with T, and C with G. The order of these pairs of molecules, called DNA sequences, creates the code for our genetic makeup. Using the analogy of a ship, the DNA code is the blueprint that determines whether the ship is a pleasure craft, tugboat or ocean liner."

Dr. Carmody had a tugboat design and a grouchy personality. But maybe he hadn't always been that way. I started speculating. Could his lifestyle choices have altered his DNA? In Aspects of Aging, he taught us that diet and exercise were largely responsible for our health. Could his habits have changed his traits, his health and even how fast he aged? I was getting pretty far out, but I wanted to give Dr. Carmody the benefit of the doubt. I didn't want to believe he was ill. I leaned forward in my chair, eager to hear whatever was coming.

"DNA segments that carry genetic information are called genes," he said.

A young man shot his hand up. "What does DNA look like?"

"DNA looks like two intertwined strands of a rope. Parts of each strand include the four molecules A, T, C, and G, paired up in various sequence," he said. "After scientists discover the order of some of these pairs in DNA segments, they share their findings with other scientists, because the complete set of human DNA, called the human genome, has about three billion base pairs."

No wonder it could take fifteen years to map the genome.

Meredith raised her hand. "Where is the DNA?"

"Every cell in the human body has DNA, except for red blood cells. In the center of each cell are twenty-three pairs of chromosomes with tens of thousands of genes inside them which make up the DNA."

Locating specific genes must be like looking for needles in a haystack. How miraculous that humans have genes similar enough to be identified; yet billions of molecules interact to produce unique human beings.

Dr. Carmody took a deep breath and put his hands against the desk to steady himself. His effort was taking a toll. He plopped in his chair, swiped his hand across his mouth, grabbed a tissue to wipe his perspiring forehead and took several sips of water. We waited to see if he could continue. I was surprised when he smiled.

"We are very fortunate at UHT," he said, "to be one of the universities participating in the Human Genome Project. All the universities and labs working together on the project are about halfway through decoding the order of three billion base pairs. The Human Genome Project should be completed by 2005."

My mind wandered to the future. That would be eight years from now. By 2005, Sam and I could be happily married. Or I might be a decrepit, lonely hag, wallowing in oblivion. I'd better learn all I could about the genetics of aging.

"Let's take a break," he said with a heavy sigh.

I hoped after the break he could continue.

Three

Meredith and I padded to the hall.

"He's really good, isn't he?" she said between sips of water.

"Fantastic. I wish I hadn't disrupted his class last semester. I didn't mean to. When I don't understand, I simply have to ask questions until I do."

"It's probably genetic, Aggie."

"Probably. Why should he get upset over questions? He undoubtedly knows all the answers."

When we filed back into the room, Carmody hadn't budged. He cleared his throat and gathered himself to resume lecturing.

"When scientists study aging, they use organisms that don't live very long. Microscopic roundworms, called *C. elegans*, have simple body processes, easily manipulated genes, and a lifespan of two to three weeks."

I wondered what tiny roundworms had to do with anti-aging.

Dr. Carmody explained. "Researcher Cynthia Kenyon showed that altering the worms' daf-2 gene affected their 'downstream' genes. This allowed them to live twice as long as roundworms lacking the genetic mutation. The mutated daf-2 gene, they discovered, regulated not only aging, but also affected the worms' resistance to stress, their metabolism and their development—all factors associated with aging."

I was ecstatic. These results were exactly what I wanted to hear. Scientists could eventually apply what they learned about roundworms to search for similar genetic processes in humans.

Sam and I could have long, healthy lives to enjoy each other, which was good since we were getting a late start. Everyone could live longer, more productive lives. I could be learning about a breakthrough in this very class that would change the course of humanity. My skin prickled with goosebumps.

Carmody, spent from his effort, spread deeper into his chair and ran a shaky finger down the paper on his desk. "Let's take this opportunity to learn about our fellow classmates," he said, as if he needed an excuse to take a longer break.

I looked around. Our classmates were quite a variety. Tall, skinny professorial types, a middle-aged woman dressed to appear twenty (it wasn't working), a girl with a skirt awfully short to wear to class, two young men who might be graduate or postgraduate students, and a batch of undergrads dressed in 1990s grunge...their last chance to look cool before they had to don interview garb and mold themselves into the next century.

Across the classroom, a lean, bespectacled forty-ish man raised his arms, stretched back in his chair and pressed his head into his palms, a satisfied expression on his face. He looked too old to be a student. But then again, so did I. Maybe he was participating with Carmody in the genome project.

Carmody stopped at a name. "Penelope Farquhar. Why don't you introduce yourself?" He picked up an Afrin bottle, sprayed his nose and dabbed the cavernous entrance with Kleenex.

Penelope stood slowly as if to make sure everyone appreciated her importance. Her Rachel haircut, straight and smooth, was a trendy choice for her mid-forties face. I wondered if she watched *Friends* and reruns of *That Girl*. A blue denim jacket covered her flowered shirt.

My t-shirt and warm-up pants weren't exactly fashionable. I was dressed for after-class, youth-preserving exercise. In case I felt the urge.

"I write for *Modern Maturity*," Penelope announced. "I studied cellular biology, so I try to give readers up-to-date information on staying young."

The magazine was published by AARP, the American Association of Retired Persons. The publication's mission appeared to be buoying up innocent souls who turned fifty before they knew what hit them.

"So far, my studies make me think that diet and exercise can cause people's genes to change," Penelope said.

Maybe my thought about lifestyle being capable of changing genetics wasn't so far-fetched after all. Penelope lifted her chin and looked around as if inviting challenges. Nobody responded, so she plopped into her chair.

Carmody, pale and expressionless, gazed into space, then flipped his hand toward the bespectacled man. "Eric," he said, "tell them who you are."

Eric unfolded himself in sections to a height over six feet. He ran his fingers through thinning hair.

"I'm Eric Lager, Dr. Carmody's research assistant. I did postdoctoral research at the University of Texas Health Science Center, then came here to work with Dr. Carmody. We hope to contribute to the genome project."

I hoped Dr. Carmody could still direct the research.

"Tell them what we do in the lab, Eric."

"We cut pieces of DNA into fragments, take the fragment containing our gene of interest and put it into a plasmid that allows us to make copies. We mutate some of the copied genes. Then we study the normal version of the gene versus the mutated versions."

Students frowned, trying to fathom the concept that scientists could actually change genes.

"We ask ourselves these questions," Eric said. "Will our modifications cause disease? Can we alter a gene to prevent disease? Can modified DNA delay aging? We try to determine which gene variants or mutations cause disease or deterioration and how we might change those mutations to produce beneficial effects."

He continued. "Studying the genetic makeup of all organisms is the purpose of genetic research. Changing somebody's DNA through gene therapy, even to cure a fatal genetic disease, differs from traditional medical remedies, so it's frightening to some people. Assuming we could insert altered DNA back into an organism, how would it affect the organism?" He attempted to smile. His lip curled.

The implications of what Eric said hit me. I jumped up. "Are you saying that after you insert substances into DNA to change genes in the lab, you can insert altered DNA back into people and change their genetic makeup?"

Eyes snapped toward me as though I'd crashed a cymbal.

A student to my right leaned toward me and whispered from the corner of his mouth, "That's sort of what happens in the movie *Gattaca*."

Eric Lager stared at me, his brow furrowed. Carmody stood, raised one arm like a rifle and pointed it straight at me.

"Don't imply we're into witchcraft here. We conduct legitimate scientific inquiry with the betterment of mankind uppermost in our minds!" His face turned red and he wobbled. "What are you doing in here anyway, Amanda...Augusta?"

It was not the right moment to correct him about my name.

Meredith popped up, a blond spire. "Aggie didn't mean to imply anything. She was just trying to clarify the purpose of research done here."

Carmody turned redder by the second. Eric grasped his arm to steady him and lowered him into the chair. I felt uneasy, like I was watching my brilliant professor about to detonate.

"Are you feeling bad again, Professor? Take it easy. Must be your allergies. Sit comfortably for a few minutes. I'll take over until the end of class."

Carmody nodded, his mouth slack. Eric stood in front of Carmody's desk, obscuring the professor's face. Carmody's broad outline bulged from behind the skinny research assistant.

Eric, trying to appear relaxed, started to loll on the edge of Dr. Carmody's desk. He stopped when a woman jutted her head inside the classroom door.

"Did I hear Dr. Carmody shouting?" Her voice was high and strained. "Is something wrong?"

Four

Eric straightened to face the formidable woman planted in the doorframe. With her gray shirtdress, gray-striped brunette hair stretched back into a bun, pewter-framed glasses and bulky black tennis shoes, she resembled a concrete pillar with a bobble head. With effort, she could be attractive. She apparently preferred to focus on her intellectual image.

"No, no, Dr. Bigsby. We're fine," Eric Lager explained. "We're having a lively discussion about DNA."

Her gaze flew to Carmody.

Eric continued, "He stood outside in the heat before class. His allergies are acting up. They're even worse than mine. He and I are teaching class together."

Eric stepped between Carmody and Bigsby and extended his hand toward her. "May I introduce Dr. Hortense Bigsby, chair of the biology department."

Hortense looked uncomfortable but tried to smile. "Hello, everyone." She was already backing into the hall. "Carry on. Carry on."

Meredith and I sank into our chairs. I hadn't intended to start a ruckus. Thank goodness my logical friend defended me.

"Dr. Carmody said we'd delve deeper into the genetics of aging," Eric said, checking his watch. "Maybe we should save that for another class."

A young woman with spiked hair and lashes heavy with mascara batted her eyes at Eric. Grateful for the distraction, he smiled at her.

"Brandy, uh, Barbara," he corrected himself. "Why don't you introduce yourself?"

"I'm Barbara Crystal. I work in Dr. Carmody's lab as assistant to Eric Lager." Her pixie haircut spiked at intervals. Her dark-rimmed eyes were almost the size of her hoop earrings. A neon yellow t-shirt pasted her body. Below her miniskirt, she wore black opaque tights, slouch socks and white sneakers. How much did she know about Dr. Carmody's experiments?

"My parents are professors. Seems like everybody in Boston is either a student or professor. I got my doctorate there under Dr. Carmody, so I decided to move here and help him in the lab. It's awfully far from Boston. This heat is suffocating, and we're miles from the initial Genome Project. But Dr. C and Eric have made progress deciphering genetic effects of aging, so who knows?"

She shrugged, suggesting that nothing important could come from outside the East Coast. She had reluctantly agreed to give the hinterlands a shot.

"Friends call me Brandy," she added, then sat back down.

Other students introduced themselves, but after Brandy, no one was memorable. I was curious about the men who identified themselves as postdoctoral scientists. One, Stanley something, said he was interested in telomeres, whatever those were. The other man, Phillip, was interested in APOE genes linked to Alzheimer's disease. They must be familiar with Dr. Carmody's research, but they were vague about how closely they worked with him.

Eric pointed a bony finger at Meredith. "How about you, Ms. Laughlin? Meredith, is it?"

She stood. "I'm in the liberal arts graduate program at UHT studying counseling to help young people. With biologists making life-changing discoveries so fast, it will undoubtedly change our counseling perspective." She smiled and took her seat.

"Indeed." Eric turned to me. His smile vanished. "Ms. Mundeen. Agatha?" He'd saved me for last. Carmody leaned forward and glared. I stood, feeling vulnerable and crummy in my t-shirt and warm-up pants.

"Actually, I go by Aggie. I'm a graduate liberal arts major too, and I'm fascinated by the aging process. I write the newspaper column 'Stay Young with Aggie.' My readers want to know about current research that might keep them young. I'm looking for revelations to inspire them."

Penelope snapped her head in my direction. Did she think we were in competition for AARP articles?

"Well, Agatha," Eric said, "I hope we rise to your expectations." I watched his lip curl and tried to decide if it was fish or frog-like.

Dr. Carmody stretched his neck and pinned me with beady eyes. I was afraid he remembered my disrupting his previous class.

Eric turned toward him. "We'll delve more into genes and telomeres next week, right, Professor?"

Carmody nodded, grabbed the Afrin bottle and sprayed his nose. I'd never seen anybody use Afrin so frequently, especially when it didn't seem to help.

"Before class ends," he said with a sniff, "I'll have Eric pass out sheets with contact numbers for me and class members in case anyone has questions or wants to form study groups. Before Thursday's class, I want you to study the history of genetics. You'll see how mystifying diseases used to be. Conditions befell people and their children that were frightening and incomprehensible."

Drained from the effort, Dr. Carmody slumped in his chair. "Genetic associations with disease have proven nothing short of amazing." He grew pale and licked his lips. Watching him loosen his collar and struggle to inhale, I was surprised he'd made it to the end of class.

He stood unexpectedly, and Eric took his arm. Carmody's brow popped with sweat. Liver-red coloration rose from his chins. He appeared confused, searching the room for someone he recognized. When his gaze settled back on Eric, he seemed comforted and sat.

As soon as Meredith and I received our contact sheets, we bolted into the hall.

"See what I mean?" I whispered. "He barely made it through one lecture." I was dying to talk to other students to see if they knew what was wrong with our professor.

"Maybe it's the heat. Or a temporary bug," she said.

"I think it's more than heat. He loses and regains concentration like there's something wrong with his brain. Hey, thanks for defending me."

"Sure. He almost flew off the handle." We bounced down the steps.

"I have to learn to phrase questions so Dr. Carmody doesn't feel challenged," I said.

"Good luck. Feeling awful must make him argumentative."

"I guess his allergies are the reason he keeps squirting that spray up his nose. He'd need a fire hose to get something far enough up that schnozzle." I chuckled and immediately felt guilty. Worrying about him was making me snarky. "What if he can't tolerate me the whole semester, no matter how diplomatic I manage to be? What if he gets sicker? Becomes irrational?"

"Why worry about a lot of what-ifs?"

She was disgustingly logical.

"Because this class means everything to me. I hinted in my column that I'd reveal anti-aging breakthroughs."

"Tell me you didn't do that."

"I did. And my editor noticed. If I don't come through, I could lose my job."

"Oh, Aggie."

There was another reason this class meant so much. I wanted to stay young for Detective Sam Vanderhoven. Meredith knew I was attracted to him, but I hadn't told her I was in love with him and determined we'd spend the rest of our lives together. Actually, I hadn't told him either. There was a secret from my past I hadn't mentioned. I had to be sure he loved me before I confessed. And I wasn't sure how long it would take me to get around to that.

My chances to accomplish anything were looking shaky.

Five

I could hardly wait to get home. When Meredith dropped me off, I flew inside, slapped a turkey and cheese sandwich together, and sat down at the computer to click through articles Dr. Carmody had listed about the history of genetics.

Could some genetic anomaly be causing his illness? I had no medical training, but maybe I'd come across symptoms like his in my studies to suggest what could be wrong with him. I loved sleuthing, and tracking down the insidious malady overtaking my professor was like sleuthing for a killer. Using the investigative approach would at least give me impetus to study and make me feel like I was helping him.

I read about all sorts of rare disorders, first discovered because doctors noticed similar symptoms appearing in patients for which they had no explanation. For example, author Pearl S. Buck, Pulitzer Prize winner for *The Good Earth*, delivered a daughter in 1920 who failed to develop normally and grew up mentally impaired with no apparent cause.

Thirty years later, scientists observed similar symptoms in other children and realized that Pearl Buck's child and others had PKU, a condition caused by inheriting defective copies of the PAH gene from both parents. The genes caused a protein-making substance to build to destructive levels and cause children's intellectual disabilities. Once they pinpointed the cause, scientists developed PKU infant formulas that provided amino acids for nutrition but kept damaging substances low enough to preserve children's brain function.

How devastating to have a debilitated child without knowing the reason or source, and be completely unable to help. I thought about my own child. She wasn't born with a genetic disease. Yet I had lost her twice.

The genetic anomalies I read about were discovered in children and couldn't apply to Dr. Carmody. But there were diseases with genetic components that appeared later in life: cancers, Alzheimer's disease and schizophrenia. Scientists believed these diseases came from multiple genetic mutations, lack of vital substances in the body or an accumulation of disease-causing agents. There were so many possible causes for these diseases that scientists hadn't investigated them all.

I couldn't learn enough to help Dr. Carmody. But maybe I could help readers. I sorted through my mail and found a letter addressed to Dear Aggie.

Dear Aggie,

I'm fifty and divorced. I gave my best years to my husband and young family. My children grew up, my husband and I grew apart, and all I see in my future is growing old.

Desperate in Dodge City,
Dorothy

Dear Desperate Dorothy,

There is indeed a Yellow Brick Road! New paths open up every day. In my Science of Aging class, I've already learned that scientists are working to alter genes to cure or prevent disease. And they've linked specific genes to aging. Yes, you heard right. Don't give up hope. Fifty is the new thirty. Take care of your health. Practice your smile. You ain't seen nothin' yet!

Skipping down the Yellow Brick Road,
Aggie

Feeling hopeful, I decided to search for information about the movie *Gattaca*. I realized the producer had created the title using abbreviations for the four DNA molecules, A, T, C, and G.

In the story, future scientists could identify genes for every human trait. By combining the perfect set of genes, they could clone a perfect human being.

The story's main character, "genetically inferior" Dreamer, was obsessed with going into outer space, but only "genetically perfect" people were eligible. His "genetically perfect" friend, who had suffered a spinal cord injury, couldn't apply for the mission. He provided Dreamer with blood, urine, and tissue samples so he could ace his genetics tests and apply.

The story showed that the human spirit could transcend genetics. *Gattaca* would be released in October. I decided to use the storyline for a future column and started scribbling:

Dear Readers,

When you watch the movie Gattaca, *don't be led into thinking that cultivating a genetically perfect human is on the horizon. It's not. But scientists have already located hundreds of genes that cause diseases. With human genome projects in full swing, they are now locating genes that affect aging. Stay tuned and stay hopeful.*

Excited,
Aggie

I didn't feel quite as hopeful as I let on, since I was pretty sure something was seriously wrong with Dr. Carmody. Surely someone would be able to help him.

Six

By the time we took our seats for Thursday's class, I had a zillion unanswered questions. Carmody, with his spray and tissue handy, scanned the room and steeled himself to lecture. In addition to taking notes, I'd decided to make a list of his obvious symptoms. I wasn't medically qualified, but it was the only way I knew to help. We'd had our differences, but we made peace, and I didn't like watching him suffer.

Eric Lager occupied his seat among the students, looking smug, as if he'd been involved with Carmody's discovery. I adopted an intellectually eager expression, trying not to stare at Carmody's nose hairs. He launched into his lecture with a strong voice.

"I know you've been studying how faulty genes can cause diseases. By now you're probably wondering how your millions of genes could possibly have produced a normal human being."

We nodded.

"Many of you are also wondering if you should undergo genetic testing, especially if you plan to have children."

More nods. I glanced at Meredith, wondering if she'd ever remarry and ponder that question.

"Let me make a few points about genetic testing," Carmody said. "The ability to detect genetic mutations is quite different from being able to positively identify a gene that causes a disease."

I knew it was none of my business, but I couldn't help wondering if doctors told him he had a genetic mutation that caused his symptoms.

"A gene mutation," he said, "even if it can be modified, cannot always stop a disease."

He continued. "People considering having genetic testing should ask: 'If I have a gene mutation associated with a disease, can the disease be prevented or treated? Are the genes tested the only ones that cause a particular condition?'"

Drained from his effort, Dr. Carmody slumped into his chair. It had taken four minutes of lecturing to wear him out. I wrote it down.

He took a deep breath.

I scribbled, "Needs oxygen." I wondered if he'd had any chest pain from clogged arteries that limited the amount of oxygen getting to his brain.

"Now, let's define aging," he said. "Scientists describe aging as the progressive decline of an organism's tissue function that eventually results in mortality. Cells become unable to function or lose their ability to replicate." His expression grew sad. "It's important to note that aging varies between individuals and is not a disease."

That was one way to look at it. If you weren't a single woman catapulting toward middle-age.

Dr. Carmody appeared spent. Dr. Eric Lager stood and began to lecture. "Scientists have made another important discovery about aging."

Was he going to reveal the discovery he and Carmody had made? I sat straighter.

"At the ends of our chromosomes are telomeres," he said. "Like plastic tips on shoelaces, telomeres protect our chromosomes, which hold our genetic data.

"Our cells, which house these chromosomes, have to divide so we can grow new skin, blood, bone and other cells when needed. But each time a cell divides, telomeres on the ends of chromosomes get shorter. When they get too short, cells can no longer divide, and they become inactive or die. Short telomeres have been associated with aging, cancer and a higher risk of death."

This was scary. Now we had to worry about the length of our telomeres.

"If a person's telomeres are really short," he said, "cells begin to die. But the human enzyme called telomerase can lengthen telomeres. Telomerase can also cause dying or inactive cells to change and become potentially immortal. Unfortunately, cancerous cells are also frequently immortal."

My classmates and I looked around at each other in confusion. I couldn't just sit there—I had to understand the effect of telomerase on telomeres. When my hand shot up, Penelope Farquhar whipped her head around and glared.

"So telomerase can cause telomeres to lengthen and protect cells, which is good. But it can also change cells so they divide unregulated and become cancerous cells? Is that right?" I asked, hoping for a more detailed explanation.

Eric Lager looked at Carmody and waited for him to respond. Dr. Carmody blinked with the same confused look he exhibited at our first encounter.

Lager answered, "That is correct. Telomerase inhibitors are sometimes used to treat cancers because they keep cells from dividing." He looked back at Carmody. "Are you all right, Professor?"

Carmody blinked, then stared intently at Eric Lager, as if trying to recall something about him.

"Eric...Yes. I'm fine." He put both hands on the desk to steady himself, squinted, stared at his notes and sniffed a couple of times. "Let's see." He swiped the back of his hand across his mouth. "Where were we?"

"We're discussing how telomerase can have either a good or bad effect on telomeres."

"Ah, yes," Carmody said. "So unpredictable. Will telomerase kill cancer cells and sustain life, or will it hasten death? Will propanolol, the drug so many people take to lower their blood pressure, lower the pressure or make a person unable to breathe?"

Students frowned at each other, bewildered.

Carmody continued. "Studies have found shortened telomeres in many cancers: pancreatic, bone, lung, kidney, head and neck, bladder, prostate..."

He pointed to corresponding areas of his body. Fortunately, he skipped prostate.

What did Dr. Carmody suffer from?

He raised his arms in supplication to the class as if begging us to respond to some unanswered question. Then his expression grew militant. He shook a pointed finger. "But when scientists have used telomerase in lab experiments to make human cells keep dividing far beyond their normal limits, the cells do *not* become cancerous!"

My hand started to rise. Eric Lager leaned in my direction and glared. I lowered my hand, but my feet started itching—an annoying quirk that occurred when curiosity overwhelmed me.

Carmody raised his voice. "What if we could immortalize cancer-free human cells in the lab and transplant them into people?"

Was that even possible? Students grew very still.

"We could grow insulin-producing cells for diabetics," Carmody shouted. "New nerve cells for muscular dystrophy. Cartilage cells for arthritics. We could grow an unlimited supply of human cells and inject perfect cells into whoever needs them!" His face turned red.

My hand shot up. "Could you actually do that? In the lab?" I didn't intend to shout.

Penelope Farquhar, Eric Lager and Brandy Crystal stared at me with threatening eyes, commanding me to be quiet. The two postdocs shrank in their chairs.

I detected motion at the front of the room. Carmody was teetering. Eric whirled and reached toward him. Carmody's red face turned purple as he pointed at me, apparently attempting to answer.

No words came from his mouth. Penelope's hands flew to her face, as if she couldn't bear to watch. Brandy sprang from her chair but froze to the spot.

Eric talked quietly to Carmody and sat him down. The purple hue left Carmody's face. His red flush subsided. He seemed to have recovered and, thank goodness, forgotten about me.

Eric dismissed class. Everyone filed out except for Carmody, Eric, and Brandy. Everybody else shunned the chaotic scene and fled toward the stairs, with Meredith and me right behind the pack.

Before we reached the stair rail, we heard a thump, followed by shouts and screams. We rushed back to the classroom. Carmody had fallen to the floor. His feet poked into the hallway. I tiptoed closer to peer past his feet, over his paunch and up to his nose hairs. No air moved them. Blood had drained from his face. I thought my professor was dead.

I looked at Meredith through blurry eyes. Her hand covered her mouth. When her teary eyes met mine, she nodded.

Department Chair Hortense Bigsby rushed up. "What happened?"

"Call 911," Eric said. "I think he's had a stroke or a heart attack."

Brandy thrust a finger toward me. "If he did," she yelled, "*she* made him have it. She wouldn't leave him alone!"

Seven

The squeal of an EMS siren jarred us from shock. The class moved in a herd toward the stairs with me and Meredith in the middle. Hortense Bigsby led the pack, propelling spindly legs down the steps like Olive Oyl chasing Popeye, apparently intent on finding EMS and directing them to Dr. Carmody.

On our sprint toward the parking lot, Meredith and I saw the emergency van and passed Dr. Bigsby talking to two men carrying a stretcher. We didn't slow down. We'd seen EMS try to save people more times than anyone could wish. I hoped this team could help Dr. Kermit Carmody. The world-renowned expert on the genetics of aging, a hair's width from discovering anti-aging secrets for mankind, had been struck down.

Meredith yanked open the door of her Taurus, hopped in, let down the windows, turned on the AC, cranked the motor and sat there.

"I'm afraid he just died," she said.

I slid into the passenger side, stunned. "Maybe EMS can save him." We swiped tears from under our eyes.

We were trying to be positive, but we'd seen dead people before. To us, Dr. Carmody looked dead.

She took a deep breath and eased the car back. "Let's get moving. How devastating to collapse in front of his class. What Brandy said to you was dreadful."

"I shouldn't have shouted. But Dr. Carmody was shouting. I got caught up in the excitement of what he was saying."

"I know."

EMS would do all they could until they got him to a hospital. How could he die so suddenly? He was relatively young, brilliant, with the potential to stall the ravages of age for mankind. I couldn't process what I'd just seen.

Meredith struggled to reach back for her practical self. "If he's gone, I suppose they'll have to get somebody else to teach the class."

"Nobody knew as much as Carmody. He undoubtedly had ideas about where genetic research was headed—he may have discovered revelations about the causes of aging nobody else even thought of." I remembered my dear Aunt Novena and Uncle Fred who were already gray-haired by the time I was twelve. How much more youthful they could have been.

"What if he confided his ideas to someone?" I said. "The person he told could steer their research in the direction Carmody discovered. Without any competition." I swiveled toward her. "What if Carmody didn't die of a stroke or heart attack?"

"You mean, what if EMS can save him?"

"No. I mean, what if he died of something else?"

"Some other terrible disease?"

"What if he didn't die of natural causes?"

"You mean, what if somebody killed him? Come on, Aggie. You've been spending too much time with Sam. Why would anybody do that? Everybody wanted him to succeed. He could be the one person who could help everybody in the world stay young."

I thought about my neighbor, Grace. At sixty, she was ready to live forever.

"What if somebody was jealous of his work?" I said. "A competitor."

"I think they'd collaborate with him. Not bump him off."

"There are a slew of scientists around here: Eric, Brandy, Penelope, Dr. Bigsby, and the postdocs in class. They probably knew what he was working on. There might be others. I wasn't paying attention to everybody's background. There are scientists in the biology and chemistry departments we haven't even met. I need to find out who they are and chat with them."

"Aggie, if Dr. Carmody died or they can't save him and you snoop into his death, Sam will be furious. If you're right that somebody tried to murder Dr. Carmody, tell Sam your suspicions. He has a whole police department to find out who did it."

She pulled up to my bungalow on Burr Road. Sam had parked his car in the driveway behind my Wagoneer.

"Speak of the devil."

"Great. You can tell him your theory. Let's pray that Dr. Carmody pulls through. If they have a class next Tuesday, I'll see you then. Meanwhile, we can try to get back to normal so we can make sense of this gobbledygook about genes and telomeres." She drove off.

Eight

My pulse quickened. It always did when I saw Sam. There were conflicting reasons for that. I'd fallen in love with him, but I knew that having lost his wife and daughter in a car crash, he was skittish about getting involved. After three years, he still struggled with their loss, but I could tell he was attracted to me. He simply couldn't reconcile how he felt about me with his loyalty to his deceased loved ones.

He followed me to my front door. My hand shook a little when I turned the key in the lock, but I didn't think he saw it. I walked inside, remembering every detail of the few times he'd kissed me. We had a good chance, Sam and I, of getting together, if only life could proceed in the foreseeable future without destructive incidents or calamitous accidents. We seemed to have trouble with that.

Seeing a man die made me realize how precarious life was. Sam and I should be free to love each other while we were young. He was forty-seven. Young enough. On the cusp of forty, I was determined not to let traumatic incidences from my past prevent me from loving him.

He ambled behind me wearing his usual khaki shirt and pants. His oddly patterned tie would confuse even Rorschach. I couldn't believe I'd begun looking forward to seeing which garish tie he selected. When he turned me around and clasped my arms, my stomach fluttered.

"Aggie, I hear your professor fell out after class today."

"Word travels fast." I longed to grab him and hold on.

"The doctor at the hospital pronounced him dead. We'll talk with the EMS crew, but I'd like to hear your take on what happened."

Meredith and I were right. Carmody was dead. My heart sank as I slid into the nearest chair. Reality set in. The professor I idealized for his knowledge was actually gone. Added to the shock of seeing my professor collapse, I feared that my hopes for a future with Sam had also crashed to the floor.

I tried to describe what happened. "Dr. Carmody seemed confused when I talked to him before class last Tuesday. He remembered me, and then he didn't. You may recall we had conflicts when I took his previous class."

"Uh-huh."

"I thought that was the reason he had trouble remembering me. But after he started lecturing, he grew disoriented. His research assistant, Dr. Eric Lager, had to take over class. Today, Carmody started strong, but he seemed to feel progressively worse. He made nonsensical statements that confused us. His voice rose louder and louder. He grew so excited that when I asked him a question, my voice was loud too."

"Uh-huh."

"He turned purple and tried to answer me, but he couldn't speak. Eric calmed him and sat him down, and I thought he'd be okay. Class ended, and we left. But we heard screams, raced back and found Carmody lying on the floor. He was so pale and still that I thought he was dead."

"The doctor said EMS thought he was dead when they got there."

"Meredith and I didn't think they'd be able to help him."

"They couldn't."

I decided to hint that Carmody's death might not be accidental. "He seemed to be suffering from some awful condition. There are several scientists in class and others in the biology and chemistry departments. It's possible somebody knows what was wrong with him."

"We'll talk to his doctor and to scientists on campus. The ME's autopsy will determine what killed him, but your classmates might also be helpful. Do you know any of them?"

"Not really. They said their names, but I don't know much more." I looked at the floor.

He took my shoulders, drew me upright and leaned close to my face. "What else, Aggie?"

"A girl, Brandy Crystal, an assistant to Eric Lager in Carmody's lab, said my shouting a question caused his collapse."

"I don't believe that. Do you?"

"Not really."

He kissed my forehead and wrapped me in a hug.

I was so wrought up. I felt like a stone statue.

He felt my tension and backed away. But he held on to one shoulder. "You've had a shock." He rubbed his temple. "We see so many bodies in homicide." He dropped his arm and went to sit on the couch.

I'd tensed up before with Sam. Whenever he'd hold me or kiss me, the repulsive image of Lester and me from years earlier would appear inside my head, like a scene from a seedy movie, and I'd freeze. I was afraid trauma had stunted my sexual response— another secret about me that Sam didn't know.

He got back to business. "We'd better interview the other scientists."

With the list of names and phone numbers Carmody had passed around, I could contact the students pretty fast. My good sense struggled against my desire to be first to investigate why Carmody had died. Fortunately, good sense won. I picked up my notebook, walked to my copy machine and made a duplicate for Sam.

"Here's a list of my classmates' phone numbers. If you don't reach them, I'm sure registration can give you their addresses." I hoped registration was as sluggish as usual. "If he didn't have a stroke or heart attack," I added, "one of them might know what was wrong."

"What do you mean?"

"If something else caused his death. Some substance."

"You mean if somebody killed him? Why would you think that?"

I shrugged. "I don't know. It's just a thought. There's probably all sorts of weird stuff in that lab, and he kept acting like he didn't feel well. Maybe he accidentally inhaled something."

"I think you've been around me too long. Wasn't he overweight and out of shape?"

I took a deep breath and let out a sigh. "Yes. And he apparently had terrible allergies. He was always squirting spray up his nose."

"I better let you rest and get something to eat. You've had quite a day."

"Okay." I wanted him to leave. If Dr. Carmody died of unnatural causes as I suspected, my student status could help me break open the investigation. When I tried to help Sam investigate, it drove him crazy. But I couldn't help it. I was curious and believed wrongs should be made right. At least we had that much in common. If I could solve a crime, maybe he'd be less irritable about my help and consider me an equal. I sensed this was not the time to suggest I was the ideal person to assist him.

"Aggie."

"Yes?"

"Tell me you don't intend to get involved in investigating Carmody's death."

"I want to try and forget about it. I just want to learn about the science of aging." My eyes filled and my feet started itching.

"Stick with that plan. I like young, healthy women."

That was the last thing I wanted to hear.

He winked, kissed my forehead and walked out the door.

Nine

Sam's lingering kisses tingled like cinnamon gum. I wiped away a tear that unexpectedly slid down my face. I couldn't even be honest with Sam. When would I stop letting my past sabotage me? I was my own worst enemy.

The only way I knew to regain control and stop dwelling on my neurotic frozen responses was to use my left brain and immerse myself in studying. I plopped down at the computer.

Carmody wasn't the first obese middle-aged man to keel over from a stroke or heart attack. Why should I suspect somebody killed him? I entered his symptoms into my web crawler: shortness of breath, mental confusion (possibly from clogged arteries in his brain), obesity, occasional nasty disposition. Okay, the last one wasn't a symptom. But it was stress-related, which contributed to strokes and heart attacks. Surely he wasn't careless enough to inadvertently ingest something in the lab. Did some substance in his home make him sick? Something in the cafeteria? School food was notoriously lousy. In the teacher's lounge? Slipped into his Coke by a jealous colleague?

A killer would have to have motive. Why would somebody want to kill Dr. Carmody? What if Carmody had learned to mutate the gene that set off a biological chain reaction to delay aging? He would have been a hero, maybe a Nobel Prize winner. Another scientist could learn how to mutate that particular gene and make it possible for everyone in the world to stay younger and healthier.

But only if Dr. Carmody was out of the way.

If I managed to interview the scientists from class before Sam did, I'd find out what each one thought Dr. Carmody was working on. Academic jealousy was a powerful motive. Especially with a world-changing breakthrough in sight and fame and fortune a breath away.

Dr. Carmody had terrible allergies, but something else wrecked havoc with his system. Eric, Brandy, Penelope and the postdocs would be apt to know which lab chemicals were the most toxic.

Sam once showed me how to use Netscape to use a reverse telephone directory. Using students' names and phone numbers, I could find their addresses.

I started with the postdoctoral students, found Stanley Bly on the contact sheet and clicked his phone number into the reverse directory. It showed his former address in Manhattan near Columbia University, and a current address at Garden Apartments, San Antonio, which were UHT's on-campus apartments provided for adjunct or visiting professors. He was interested in telomeres and would know which chemicals were used to research them. I made a note to talk with Stanley Bly.

The phone number for Phillip Delay listed a former address in Manhattan, but no subsequent or current address. That was strange. Was he just visiting, or staying with Bly or someone else for the semester? Where did he go after he lived in Manhattan, before he came to San Antonio? With their common interest in genetics, both men must have visited Dr. Carmody's lab. Phillip Delay had said he was interested in APOE genes that scientists thought were related to Alzheimer's disease. Dr. Carmody had memory loss and confusion. Could he have had early-onset Alzheimer's? I marked Delay's name.

Carmody's family medical history would be important. I needed to talk with a family member, but I couldn't do it right away. They'd be in shock.

I typed "family diseases" into the browser to see what would come up and read about a single Venezuelan family numbering over three thousand. Every member inherited a defective gene from a common ancestor—the largest known concentration of the same disease in a single family. It took until 1993 for scientists to locate the offending gene on chromosome 4. Now tests were offered to people with a family history of degenerative Huntington's disease. Symptoms of the disease sometimes manifested themselves later in life. Dr. Carmody must have had regular medical checkups, so doctors would have discovered this disease.

I'd reached a dead end until I could interview people, so I decided to check my mail. There must be somebody I could help. Among the bills, one envelope was addressed to Dear Aggie. I tore it open.

Dear Aggie,

I'll be forty-nine this year. I can't imagine growing old and want to do everything I can to postpone it. I exercise and watch what I eat, but I read so much conflicting advice.

Confused in Chicago

Dear Confused,

The advice is confusing because scientists are making discoveries daily. I just learned we have telomeres at the end of our chromosomes. Like plastic tips on shoelaces, they protect our genetic data. If our telomeres get too short, we age and die sooner. But if our cells grow unregulated, they can become cancerous. Scientists struggle to determine how to maintain telomeres at the right length. While short telomeres have been linked to aging, no one knows whether shorter telomeres are just a sign of aging—like gray hair—or if they actually contribute to aging.

There's a lot more to learn, but take heart. Scientists are moving at warp speed.

More later,
Aggie

I couldn't bring myself to tell her that the renowned scientist who knew the most about aging, Dr. Kermit Carmody, wasn't moving at all.

Just as I emailed my letter to Confused to the *San Antonio Flash-News*, Sam called.

"I just talked to the doctor who pronounced Dr. Carmody dead."

"Okay." I closed my eyes.

"There's more, Aggie. I talked with Dr. Bigsby, the biology department chair. She heard from students you were shouting questions in class that might have contributed to Carmody having a stroke or heart attack."

"Unbelievable."

"I know you didn't cause his death, but that's the rumor floating around. I thought you should know. You need to keep a low profile in class."

I started thinking.

"Aggie? Did you hear what I said?"

"Yes. Of course. I should keep a low profile. Good idea."

While Sam changed the subject to another case he'd be working over the weekend, I decided my first interview should be with Dr. Hortense Bigsby. As department chair, if she believed I contributed to Carmody's death, she could have me dismissed from the university. I had to see her to defend myself.

"Don't work too hard, Sam. And don't worry. I'll be mouse quiet in class next week."

Ten

I hung up and padded to the kitchen for peanut butter, grape jelly and low-fat milk. Before taking the first bite, I dialed UHT. "Biology department, please. Dr. Bigsby's office."

I made an appointment through her secretary and carried the feast to my kitchen table. PB & J helped me order my thoughts. For once I was glad Aunt Novena had been a cardiac nurse who studied out loud all the time. I learned a lot from her. I scribbled on a tablet.

1. Carmody was obese, but he'd been that way for years. Why did he have a stroke or heart attack now? His erratic ability to think and remember suggested a brain impairment more than a heart disorder.

2. His symptoms came and went as though some substance in his system sporadically caused reactions. Which made me think his death was induced.

3. His behavior was symptomatic of many malfunctions. Maybe I should just wait for the ME's autopsy report.

I was not good at waiting. I thought Carmody was murdered. He was about to make a breakthrough and it got him killed.

Maybe somebody had managed to shorten the telomeres protecting his chromosomes.

To rest my brain, I watched TV sitcoms. Before bed, I returned to the computer to scan through links Carmody had provided. When I talked with Dr. Hortense Bigsby, I hoped to sound reasonably knowledgeable.

Eleven

I arrived at Dr. Bigsby's office at eight a.m. Friday morning, bleary-eyed from studying late Thursday night. Her secretary had specified the early hour, yet she hadn't arrived. I wondered if her boss would chastise her. I crossed the reception area and knocked on the door to Dr. Bigsby's office.

She uttered a weak "Yes?"

When I peeked in, I had the sensation of viewing a statue seated behind a desk.

Light from a small window gleamed on chrome-like strips of hair that looked like spokes restraining her bun. She looked both elegant and miserable, like royalty trained to contain her emotions. Her red-rimmed eyes were expressionless.

"Thank you for seeing me," I stammered. "I came to offer my condolences on our loss of Dr. Carmody. This was my second class with the professor."

"Our loss. Yes." She took a deep breath and blinked, one of two daily blinks she probably allowed herself. She might be in shock from losing her colleague.

"Have you worked with him a long time?"

"Yes. A long time. I was his student back in Boston." She reached toward a tissue box on a cabinet to the left of her desk. Her ring finger was bare. Behind the tissue box, I noticed a lone photograph.

"You were Dr. Carmody's student. How interesting. And now, as chair of the biology department, you were his boss."

"Ironic, isn't it?" She blew her nose, a single honk on the tissue before she folded it into squares. "Kermit could never be department chair. He hated administrative duties and paperwork. With him, research was everything. He had no time for anything else." She placed the tissue in her lap. "I was never into research; I fast-tracked toward a teaching career. Never married or had children."

At what point had she made that decision? I'd learned how hard it was to be without love.

"I guess I'll never have children either," I said, trying to make light of our shared situation. "At least we won't be worried about passing genes for Huntington's disease or Duchenne muscular dystrophy or cystic fibrosis to our children."

She gave me a calculating look. Was I really unconcerned about not having a family? Did I understand the genetics of these diseases or was I merely parroting something I'd read? She gazed into space and sighed, as if concluding that finding the answer wasn't worth the effort.

"They made me chair of the department," she said, "so I could ride herd on the aggressive, inquisitive types climbing the ladder."

Which one of those types could have killed Dr. Carmody?

She raised her chin and looked into space. "My job can be tedious, but it's important to keep the department functioning properly."

"Isn't that common among scientists?" I asked. "Not liking paperwork? As department chair, you can corral their efforts and make sure they stay on track and get their grant reports and renewals submitted on time. That's a valuable contribution."

She nodded.

I leaned forward and clasped my hands expectantly at the sheer excitement of scientific inquiry. "I'm so eager to learn about new discoveries about disease and aging. What did Dr. Carmody find the most interesting?"

The expression in her eyes warmed. "There is so much being discovered about how genes interact to affect disease and point to signposts of aging...and how genes can change and make cells grow uncontrolled..."

"And can lead to cancer?"

"Yes. Eighty-five percent of human cancers are telomerase positive."

"Telomerase. The enzyme that lengthens telomeres and protects the chromosomes in our DNA?"

"Yes. Dr. Elizabeth Blackburn is an amazing scientist working with telomerase. Her research sparked a whole field of inquiry into the possibility that telomerase could be reactivated to treat age-related diseases like blindness, cardiovascular disease and neurodegenerative diseases, and perhaps even be deactivated to treat cancer."

Her excitement was contagious. "Aren't some researchers focusing on the connection of Alzheimer's to specific genes? I think they're called APOE genes."

She stiffened. Her neck stretched longer than Olive Oyl's. Her head bobbled.

Her long neck, held erect and properly adorned, would make her appear regal and chic. It saddened me that she hadn't used her attributes to their best advantage. Her defensive attitude made her imposing but not elegant.

"Dr. Carmody," she stated, "did not have Alzheimer's."

"I didn't mean to imply that he did...just that scientists are investigating possible genetic causes for the disease. I thought he might have been interested in that."

"He might have been." A cloud seemed to descend over her. She sank under its weight, causing her blue cotton shirtdress to form a wrinkle over her flat bosom.

"If you were Carmody's student," I said, "you must have come to UHT after he arrived."

"I was actually here before he came. He left Boston to do postdoctoral research at Columbia."

I remembered the two postdoctoral students in my class had studied at Columbia before one of them dropped off the radar.

"I stayed in Boston to finish my dissertation," she said. "That took a while. Then I came here." She resurrected the geometrically folded tissue, puffed twice and refolded it in her lap.

"Completing your dissertation must have required tremendous focus and dedication. I commend you for earning your doctorate. And then to become a department chair so soon after obtaining your degree. It must have been a thrill to be called to this university."

Her chin rose proudly, but her eyes remained sad. "A thrill. Yes."

"Had Dr. Carmody been ill for a long time? Do you know why he died so suddenly?"

"He wasn't ill, so far I knew. He was overweight and subject to the usual stress that can strain a person's heart." An icy chill settled in her eyes.

It was time to defend myself. "I've heard that some people think my shouting caused Dr. Carmody to have a heart attack. But he was quite excited. He was actually shouting himself. He'd appeared ill and confused earlier while conducting class. I would hate to think I contributed to his demise, but I really don't think I was the cause."

"No. I suppose not."

I exhaled. I was accused, but not yet indicted.

"Lately," she said, "he seemed easily upset. It probably wasn't your fault. I encouraged him to get in shape, but..." She shrugged and sighed.

"His family must be in shock. Do they live here?"

She nodded. "His younger brother, Claude, is a financial advisor."

"Does he have other family?"

"Not that I know of."

We grew still with the realization sinking in that Dr. Carmody was gone. Forever.

"I'm so sorry," I said. My eyes misted. "If you don't mind I'll grab one of those tissues."

As I reached across the corner of her desk to pluck a tissue from the box, she recoiled backward as if to avoid human touch. The photograph behind the box pictured her and Dr. Carmody. He had no paunch. The hair on the top of his head hadn't slid backwards toward his neck. His huge nose and nostrils did suggest future prominent nose hairs. He was fairly nice-looking. I could understand why she might have worshiped him as her mentor.

Dr. Bigsby looked slim and hopeful in the picture, precursor to the graceful, accomplished lady she could become. I sniffed and reached for a second tissue, eyeballing the photo. The young Dr. Carmody looked somewhat like my classmate, Phillip Delay.

Had Doctors Carmody and Bigsby been teacher and protégé? Fellow scientists? Friends? Lovers?

That last thought threw me into a coughing fit. I used the Kleenex tissue to cover my mouth. She appeared appalled that I might be contaminating her office. I tried to stop coughing and backed toward the door.

"I'm so sorry about Dr. Carmody. Thank you for seeing me." I backpedaled through the door and bumped into her late-arriving, pasty-faced office assistant. I waved an apology to them both and escaped.

Pushing my beloved Wagoneer, Albatross, to the speed limit, I sailed home, trying to erase the nasty image that kept popping into my head of Kermit Carmody and Hortense Bigsby, naked.

The column I planned to write would require my complete concentration. It might be the last one I'd write for awhile if I got preoccupied investigating Dr. Carmody's death. I couldn't shake the belief that his death wasn't accidental. My plan was to shake the undergrowth for suspects and see who popped out.

I slipped into my garage, jumped out of Albatross and charged through the door in the garage that led to my kitchen. To lift my spirits, I smeared peanut butter on an overripe banana. Plopped in front of my computer, I combed through a few scientific articles, squished the delectable mixture around my mouth and started making an outline.

In my next "Stay Young with Aggie" column, I'd extol Dr. Carmody's professional virtues, emphasize the importance of his research and stress the magnitude of his loss to the scientific community. After doing a tad more research, I'd drop a few hints: Had Carmody been close to isolating a gene or discovering a genetic pathway that could greatly extend human life? Had he unearthed a breakthrough to cure a disease? Had he combined his research with someone else to explain genetic interactions?

After polishing the column on Friday, I'd take it to my editor at the paper. I'd secure his promise that it would appear in Monday morning's edition. My classmates would have time to read it before Tuesday's class, assuming there was a class. I planned to study their reactions.

When I thought I had enough meat in the article to entice UHT's biological wizards, I started to write.

I submitted my column on schedule to the *San Antonio Flash-News* editor.

Twelve

First thing Monday morning, I swooped the newspaper from my porch, raced inside and tore through the sections. "Stay Young with Aggie" was in the Health and Beauty section, not far from the obituaries. Dr. Carmody was eloquently featured in both. I'd included his name in my column title to catch people's eye: *Renowned Professor Dr. Kermit Carmody Unexpectedly Dies.*

His obituary stated his funeral was scheduled for Tuesday afternoon. His colleagues and my classmates would have plenty of time to absorb information from the newspaper about their beloved professor before his funeral. One university announcement took me by surprise. To honor Dr. Kermit Carmody's memory, classes would not meet Monday and Tuesday. The university would hold a private memorial gathering for university faculty and students in the auditorium of the main building Tuesday morning at ten a.m. Only guests with student or faculty IDs or affiliated researchers would be admitted. The general public was not invited.

What an opportunity. This private event would give me a chance to talk with students in my class, scientists from UHT's biology and chemistry departments and researchers who'd communicated with Dr. Carmody. I read over my newspaper article to make sure I'd included the salient points:

1. Carmody was working on telomeres, whose length coincided with longevity, and with telomerase, the enzyme that increased telomere length.

2. He was interested in how the daf-2 gene affected the expression of other genes that sped up or slowed "downstream" genes that appeared to be earmarks for aging.

3. He was interested in investigating APOE genes that appeared related to Alzheimer's disease.

I threw this in because of Dr. Bigsby's emphatic reaction, and because scientists thought APOE genes were implicated in twenty to twenty-five percent of Alzheimer's cases.

I didn't pretend to comprehend all the genetic information I tossed out, but scientists would understand it, and they'd wonder how much I knew. If one of them killed Carmody because they planned to claim credit for his ideas, that person would find my article quite interesting, and be compelled to find out what I knew. I could hardly wait for Tuesday's gathering.

Although Dr. Carmody's death was a terrible tragedy, and one the university would not easily recover from, I felt strangely optimistic. Because of my column and my association with Dr. Carmody, I might be in a unique position to flush out his killer. Maybe that would make up, in a minuscule way, for my eager questions he frequently found so disturbing.

Dr. Carmody's death, sad as it was, at least purged me from continuous mental angst about whether he would oust me from class and expel me from the university. Dr. Eric Lager would probably teach us. As Carmody's lab director, he likely knew almost as much as Carmody did. Despite my suspicions that a colleague might have stolen Dr. Carmody's secrets, I hoped his discoveries had not been lost.

Thirteen

Tuesday would be a busy day. I was vaguely apprehensive about what might happen after the memorial services, so I decided to stock up on groceries...something healthy. Whole Foods had just moved to Alamo Quarry Market. Excited about shopping for natural foods in the new facility, I donned a new t-shirt, jeans and sandals, hopped into Albatross and motored to The Quarry.

I stepped inside the store and grabbed a basket. The fresh smell was bound to clear my mind of worry and grief. Beautiful organic fruits caught my eye. I selected a combination fruit bowl and a fourteen-ounce carton of vegan fruit dip. Gazing at the tropical fruits from New Zealand, Mexico, Hawaii, Columbia and the Dominican Republic would probably give me travel dreams.

Scanning the aisles, I spied Penelope Farquhar tossing loose organic vegetables into a basket.

"Hey. Fancy meeting you here."

She gave me a semi-friendly look.

"Wasn't what happened to Dr. Carmody terrible?"

"Yes, terrible." She nodded.

"I see you like fresh vegetables," I said.

"That's what Dr. Dean Ornish says we should eat. Have you read his books?" She pivoted toward the tomatoes.

"I read the one showing that eating a diet with only ten percent fat can reverse heart disease. It's amazing."

She grabbed a red lump that looked like a cross between a beet and a potato somebody had dug up, tossed it in her basket and moved toward a bin labeled "Budock root. Japan." Foot-long stalks with three-quarter-inch diameters looked like brown bamboo. They'd make great play swords for children, except they were almost five dollars a stalk. She grabbed two.

Despite craving crunchy peanut butter, I headed for the greens and chose four kinds: red organic lettuce, arugula, butter lettuce and baby spinach. I'd read that eating greens daily could slash the risk of Type II diabetes and heart attack, protect against cancer and increase brain power. Tossing the salad with walnuts and olive oil boosted the absorption of nutrients. Why not try it? I'd ask Sam over and fix him veggie dinners before he got too old.

I ambled back toward Penelope. Since I'd run into her, I decided she'd be the subject of my first investigative interview.

"You've probably read most of Dr. Ornish's books," I said.

"I have his complete library. Want to see it? I live just over there." She pointed toward the Meridian Apartments on Basse Road.

"Sure."

My car followed hers into the gated complex. The barrier clanked closed behind us, securing us in a gloomy drive-in patio compound surrounded by high-rise apartments. We took the elevator to her third-floor unit and went in. I had the sensation of entering a sacred library of vintage books. Tall built-in bookshelves of dark wood surrounded the room. A brown leather sofa and chairs in the center circled a mahogany library table and a single straight-backed chair. Closed shutters over the only window protected the volumes and made the room even darker.

She pointed to a shelf. "There's the book you were talking about, *Dr. Dean Ornish's Program for Reversing Heart Disease.* After his patients spent only a year on his treatment program of eating a diet with ten percent fat, the narrowing of their coronary arteries decreased. Their coronary atherosclerosis was actually reversed. It was a landmark discovery. Patients who followed Ornish's regimen had fewer cardiac events than those who followed standard medical advice. Cheaper and safer therapies against cardiovascular disease could replace or eliminate coronary artery bypass surgery, angioplasty, and stents."

If Dr. Carmody had followed Dr. Ornish's regimen, would he still be alive?

"Dr. Ornish came out with *Eat More, Weigh Less* in 1993," she said.

That sounded like a great plan. "I need to read that one."

She pointed up to a third book. "*Everyday Cooking with Dr. Dean Ornish* came out in 1996 and includes a hundred and fifty recipes. The *New York Times* called it 'the most useful, accessible and inspirational cookbook yet.'"

"Wow. I see you have shelf space reserved on either side of his books." They were bracketed with expensive bookends, like a shrine.

"He'll be writing more books. I'll buy every one."

I glanced around the other shelves. I saw minimal fiction titles, a few history titles and a lot of books on biology. She stared reverently at Ornish's books.

"I ordered a pre-publication copy of his book coming out next year," I said. *Love and Survival*. The subtitle was *The Scientific Basis for the Healing Power of Intimacy*. I hoped it would help me improve my relationship with Sam, but I didn't mention it.

She didn't comment. I got the distinct impression that whatever I'd read or planned to read, she would claim to know more about the subject. I looked closer at other shelves and saw several books on living longer and extending lifespan.

"I remember you studied cellular biology," I said. "Do you read a lot about genetics?"

"Books I've read by Ornish and others suggest that only about thirty-five percent of individual differences in longevity are inherited. That leaves two-thirds of our longevity, and probably our health, dependent on how we eat, sleep, handle stress, and exercise."

"That's really something," I said. She was clearly mesmerized by Ornish.

"Some scientists," she said, "think environmental influences cause genes to respond in various ways—that a person's lifestyle can actually change his genetics. Dr. Ornish leans toward that view. If lifestyle changes can affect coronary arteries, why couldn't they affect genes associated with disease and aging?"

I nodded.

It seemed like somewhat of a leap, yet possible.

"So Dr. Ornish is not at all interested in the genetics of aging?" I began to wonder why she'd signed up for Dr. Carmody's class.

"Ornish agrees that short telomeres in humans are emerging as risk markers for disease and premature cancer deaths," she said. "He's seeking funding for a study to see whether lifestyle changes alone will increase telomere length."

"By changing your diet and exercise, you could make your telomeres grow longer?"

"Yes," she said. She seemed to have already decided the outcome of Dr. Ornish's study. Maybe she'd written articles supporting his viewpoints. If Dr. Carmody disagreed with Dr. Ornish's approach, had she viewed Dr. Carmody's research as a threat to *her* self-esteem and career? I decided to prod her a little.

"Didn't Dr. Carmody say that shortening telomeres, which speed aging, can be counteracted by the enzyme telomerase? But that too much telomerase can cause cancer?"

"Yes, he did. But Dr. Ornish thinks improved nutrition and lifestyle could increase telomerase activity, protect our immune system and combat cancer. He wants to involve other scientists in his pilot study."

Totally focused on Dr. Ornish, she could be opposed to the thrust of Dr. Carmody's research. She might even want to discredit him.

"Looks like I'll have to keep up with Dr. Ornish. I guess you believe Dr. Carmody couldn't hope to extend lifespan and improve people's health," I said, "just by mutating genes in the lab. By the way, have you been to the lab?"

She skirted the question.

"Carmody probably knew more than anyone else on the planet about the genetic components of longevity," she said, "and how to alter genes in a lab. But I believe lifestyle has a *major* effect on health and longevity. Some scientists think we have nutrient-sensing systems that respond to diet and physical activity." She sighed. I thought she was getting bored with having to explain things to me.

"Another big factor in health and longevity is emotional stress," she said pointedly, throwing me a hostile look.

I looked straight at her. "Emotional stress alone does not cause death," I stated. "Dr. Ornish says that how a person handles stress is what matters."

"I suppose so." She raised her chin. "But combined with other factors, it might cause a fatal reaction."

I wanted to get back to her beliefs. Did her credibility depend on Dr. Ornish, instead of Dr. Carmody, being on the right track?

"What do you think Dr. Carmody was particularly interested in?" I asked.

She narrowed her eyes. "Telomeres. Telomerase. Genetic mutations. Beyond that, I really couldn't say."

"I guess I'd better get this produce home," I said. "I enjoyed the visit." I whirled and headed for the door before she could say something snarky and while my eyes could still function once I reached daylight.

At home, I stuffed produce into refrigerator bins. I'd have to buy either a larger refrigerator or a rabbit. I tossed my salad, fixed iced tea and jiggled around the kitchen to the Spice Girls' "Say You'll Be There." Despite Dr. Carmody's death and Penelope's obsession, life was basically good. I concentrated on staying youthful and thought about Sam. I was pleased with my column and eager to meet Dr. Carmody's fellow scientists on Tuesday.

But first, I was going to meet Dr. Carmody's brother, Claude.

Fourteen

It wasn't difficult to find him in the phone book. There was only one Claude Carmody listed. Kermit and Claude. Under his name, I read "U.S. World Investments" with a northwest San Antonio address and phone number. His home address wasn't listed. That was okay. I probably had a better chance of seeing him without an appointment if he thought I was an investor. He might be home making funeral arrangements; I decided to call the company.

"Mr. Carmody's office, please."

His assistant came on the line.

"Hello. My name is Agatha Mundeen. I'm a new investor—in town for a few days—and thought I might make some investments while I'm here. My family lives in San Antonio, so I'm here often. I know Mr. Carmody's brother died. Such a tragedy. I wonder if he might be coming in today. I certainly don't want to impose."

"Actually, he's here now. They made funeral arrangements over the weekend, and services are tomorrow. One minute. Let me check...He says that will be fine. Can you come fairly soon? He may go home early."

"Thank you. Tell him I'm on my way."

After changing into business apparel, I hopped into Albatross, made my way to Loop 410, turned west on IH-10 and scanned the access road for the investment company. They'd probably have an imposing building with a large sign so people could find them. As expected, the company name stretched in huge letters across the top of a three-story building. I pulled into their lot, entered the expansive lobby and walked up to the girl behind an imposing information desk.

"I'm Agatha Mundeen. I have an appointment with Mr. Carmody."

"Certainly. Walk around my desk toward the rear plate glass window. His office is the last one on the right."

Under his name on the door was "Vice President, CFA, Chief Portfolio Manager." He must be the second man in charge under the CEO. As I reached for the knob, he opened the door, a salesman's smile on his face.

"Come in, come in." He grasped my hand.

"Agatha Mundeen. Thank you for seeing me on short notice. I'm so sorry about your brother."

"Thank you. It was quite sudden. Did you know him? Please, take a seat." His office was appropriate for a CEO. It had windows all across the back, mellow wood furniture upholstered with sumptuous leather, and plush carpet. I molded into the luxurious chair in front of his desk.

"I returned to graduate school and had two of my classes with Dr. Carmody. He was brilliant."

"Yes, he was. He could have made astounding discoveries. His life was cut way too short."

"Had he been ill, do you know?"

"Not to my knowledge. He didn't take care of himself...spent too much time researching and never exercised. He'd get involved with scientific inquiries and forget everything else. But ill, no."

"So he didn't take medicine for a recurring problem, perhaps some familial tendency that..."

His smile disappeared. "No. None of that. He had the usual aches and pains middle-aged people get, and he may have taken mild remedies for that. But there are no inherited diseases in our family. Now, what can I do for you?"

I'd concocted a story about wanting to spread my investments in balanced mutual funds, a few individual stocks, maybe some real estate investment trusts. He grew interested and made notes.

"I keep a bungalow here, but after your brother's funeral tomorrow, I'm going back to Corpus Christi," I said. "Shall I call you in a couple weeks to see what you recommend?"

"Perfect," he said. "I'll see you tomorrow. Thanks for coming in."

As soon as we shook hands and I left, I scooted fast as I could toward the front of the building. I'd parked Albatross on the side. I wanted to get out of the parking lot and onto IH-10 before he saw the Wagoneer. There was no way anybody who drove a car like mine could make all those investments.

Fifteen

When Meredith came to pick me up Tuesday morning for the memorial gathering, I was waiting at the curb wearing a navy pantsuit with a turned-up collar, a stylish vest and bellbottoms. We'd decided to dress for Carmody's memorial and one o'clock funeral and grab lunch between events.

"You look nice," I said. Her brown pantsuit was taller and leaner than mine. I'd gotten over longing to be tall. The best I could do was struggle to become lean.

"Thanks. So do you. Since he's famous, it'll probably be a big funeral."

"With a slew of scientists there." I wished I could wear a press pass to draw their attention.

The UHT campus looked normal when we arrived, but chatter in the first-floor hall leading to the small auditorium was subdued. People from Carmody's class shuffled like mourners. Even undergrad students wore muted attire and somber faces. They knew better than to cavort around. I recognized the postdocs from our class and slid toward them, matching their stride.

"His death is tragic, isn't it?"

Stanley Bly nodded. "Yes, tragic. We may have to search for other universities to pursue our research." The other man, Phillip Delay, nodded his head in agreement. His nose reminded me of Dr. Carmody's.

"Won't Dr. Eric Lager carry on Dr. Carmody's work?" I asked.

"Yes," Phillip said, "but he doesn't have the reputation."

Meredith caught up, and we stood in line behind the two men, waiting to be cleared for admission by one of three campus officers stationed at doors to the auditorium. I didn't have a chance to ask more questions.

A sign standing on a tripod near the middle door read: "Private Function." After the young scientists sauntered in, the officer asked to see our student identification cards.

At the next door over, a man waited for another officer to admit him. He was probably a researcher who knew Carmody but didn't have a campus ID. Stooped, with dark hair and a beard, he looked rather sinister. The officer asked for his name and address and checked it against a list. I hadn't expected so much security. The university hierarchy was obviously shaken by Dr. Carmody's untimely death. He must have been an even bigger celebrity than I imagined.

The officer looked up at the man, jerked his thumb toward the entry door, and the man trod into the auditorium. I watched where he sat so I could catch him later.

Once the officer scrutinized our ID cards, we walked in and found seats about halfway back in the auditorium. I found a paper clip in my purse and attached my name tag to the top of my collar. I told Meredith I wanted people to notice the tag so they'd come over to read it and discuss my column about Dr. Carmody's work.

She rolled her eyes. "You dropped a lot of information in that column, Aggie. You're going to get in trouble."

I grinned.

The area at the back of the auditorium was without chairs, which provided space for people to gather. Rows of chairs toward the front began to fill. They all smelled the same, these indoor corrals for gathering students: musty, tinged with an odor I imagined to be energetic hormones combined with restless feet.

Students had been summoned to participate in this interlude about death—an irrelevant condition they never expected to experience. Chomping at invisible bits, they yearned to get on with the forward motion of their lives.

On the auditorium stage in a row of chairs, middle-aged and gray-haired men and women, UHT's Board of Trustees, sat with solemn faces. Their black, gray and brown attire was similar to Dr. Bigsby's, who sat among them. In my mind's eye, learning was brightly colored, joyful, bursting with life, full of promise. When it was snuffed out, the landscape turned drab.

When the ground floor sitting area grew silent, the university president rose and walked to the podium.

"We are gathered here," President Merkel said, "to honor our fallen comrade, fellow scientist and friend, Dr. Kermit Carmody, a man whose talents were taken from us much too soon. His funeral will be held at St. Peter's Episcopal Church at one p.m. today. This gathering is a chance for you to greet one another as mutual friends of our renowned colleague and share your remembrances of him. We will now have a moment of silence in memory of our friend and associate, Dr. Kermit Carmody, after which you are free to visit among yourselves."

And try to avoid thinking about how suddenly death can overcome us.

It didn't last long—a single minute to remember a man's existence on earth. I was glad there would be a funeral service later. After a few minutes elapsed, people rose in batches and chatted, gravitating toward the back of the room while they looked for people they knew.

I headed directly to the stooped man with the shock of hair. He was looking at the floor when I approached. I stepped close enough so the ID on my collar would be in his line of vision.

"Hello. I'm Aggie Mundeen. From Dr. Carmody's Science of Aging class."

He made an effort to stand straight enough to read my ID though his bifocals. He seemed too young to be bent over. He must have spent hours leaning over test tubes.

"You're a student," he declared, trying to absorb that improbable fact. "I'm Dr. Gary Biskin, Biochemistry department, Mellencross University."

"I gather you do genetic research?"

"Yes. Primarily on BRCA1 and BRCA2 genes linked to breast cancer. We're trying to refine genetic tests offered to women who probably inherited those genes."

"Interesting. And you were a friend of Dr. Carmody's? I didn't know that was one of his fields of interest."

"Unfortunately, it wasn't. But I didn't know that until I had done massive research to prepare for my dissertation. He was on my approval committee at Columbia but was disinterested in breast cancer. Other committee members supported the direction of my inquiry, but Dr. Carmody was too involved in his own research to meet regularly with the committee. Unfortunately, he had a lot of clout. When he took time to consider my proposed research, he disapproved. I had to start over. I lost a year of work."

"He must have felt bad about that."

"Not particularly. Now, if you'll excuse me." He shuffled toward the exit.

Meredith had apparently wandered off. I recognized two stylish women I'd seen in the main building, who I thought were scientists, and sauntered over to introduce myself.

"Are you in the science department here?" I asked.

"I'm Connie Strong, from the biology department, and this is our best chemistry professor, Harriet Walker." They smiled.

"Dr. Carmody's death is such a loss. Did you work with him?"

"Well," Connie said, "we kept up with what he was doing and visited the lab, but..."

"He wasn't very communicative," Harriet finished. "When we collaborated with him on projects, we frequently didn't know the final results until he published them in a paper."

"With his name and 'colleagues' on it," Connie added. "Our names would be mentioned toward the bottom."

"That must have been frustrating."

"We sort of backed off from working with him. Sometimes we propose ideas to other labs cooperating in the genome project. Dr. Carmody had a great mind though."

Connie nodded. "We'll see you at the funeral?"

"Yes."

They smiled and walked off.

I needed to meet somebody with a positive outlook. I spotted Meredith talking to a woman wearing bright colors and four-inch heels standing with three men. She looked to be in her thirties and was smiling. The men might have been older. I walked toward the congenial group just as they left Meredith and headed toward the door. I caught up with her.

"Who were they?"

"Scientists from UT Austin—various labs. The man with the auburn beard, McIntosh, studies the daf-2 gene and its effect on 'downstream' genes. He visited with Carmody a few times. The clean-shaven man, Ted Strickland, said his lab worked with the effects of telomeres and telomerase. He talked with Dr. Carmody a lot. The sandy-haired fellow with glasses studies APOE genes and their connection to Alzheimer's."

"All the same projects Dr. Carmody was interested in. What about the lady?"

"If I understood correctly, Gretchen's lab is charting the locations of genes that scientists have identified to date. They're looking for connections, similarities, interactions or pathways between them. The men indicated that her research turned up in a paper that Carmody published."

"Ouch."

"She didn't seem perturbed. She said most of it was common knowledge."

"It's nearly noon. Let's grab Subway on our way to St. Peter's. Did you meet anybody from the biology or chemistry departments?" I asked.

"A few. I sensed more disbelief than sadness that Dr. Carmody wouldn't be around."

Sixteen

We stopped for Subway, ate while we drove to St. Peter's Episcopal Church and arrived early for the funeral. We parked in back of the church, entered the foyer, signed the guest book and tiptoed down the aisle toward the front. The first four rows were marked for family. We sat on row five. I was glad Carmody's casket was closed.

Meredith whispered in my ear, "I'm dying to see his family members."

While the organist played music so loud it made my ears ring, a woman with two teenage children arrived at the front pew, followed by Dr. Carmody's brother, Claude. Assorted people followed, probably cousins with their offspring. Professor Carmody apparently had no wife or children.

I saw a few faculty members sitting with Dr. Bigsby. Others spoke to them, scientists, I surmised, from nearby universities and research labs. I looked around for Sam but didn't see him. The UT contingent arrived and nodded to a few colleagues

The Honorable Reverend Harold McClintock, Rector of St. Peter's Episcopal Church, rose and glided to the center of the sanctuary. He had probably never seen Professor Kermit Carmody until he lay in a casket. Backed by assistant clergy and lay-people wearing long robes, he began to recite the Anglican liturgy, words created for the occasion of death, unchanged and repeated by Anglican and Episcopal worshipers through centuries.

"I am the resurrection and the life, saith the Lord; he that believeth in me, though he were dead, yet shall he live."

The lyrical, comforting words focused on man's reunion with God at death, not on humanity's loss of an individual. If a priest grew enamored of his own ad-libs, the centuries-old liturgy kept him in check. Although familiar and reassuring, the words failed to mention the deceased. Someone wandering in to pay respects would not have known who died.

Although many scientists believed in God, it was hard to imagine Dr. Carmody acquiescing to a higher power. Yet, I hadn't really known him.

Lulled by the priest's repetition of prescribed words, I began to imagine my own funeral. I hovered above, trying to determine who was thinking about me or about something else. I found it hard to capture their attention. I wanted them to know I'd sought justice and strove to be honest, loyal, loving, fair and trustworthy. Even though I didn't always succeed. I started to tear up until I remembered why I was there.

The rector lead the congregation in prayer, then read a passage from Isaiah about comforting those who mourned. Were there any? Not academic mourners, but personal mourners. I feared at least one person was not mourning.

People I scanned seemed more interested in glancing around than listening to the priest or contemplating Dr. Carmody in his casket. Stanley Bly and Phillip Delay looked back and spotted Brandy Crystal at the left end of our pew. One winked at her. The other gave her a seductive smile.

She must have applied gel to her pixie cut to control it. The spikes lay almost horizontal. Her hoop earrings were smaller than usual. I wondered if her miniskirt was longer than usual. When she glanced toward my end of the pew, I noticed her eyes were mascara-free and red-rimmed.

Had she actually cared for Dr. Carmody? Despite her disdain for his Texas work environment? Was she more than his protégé? What was her relationship to those two men?

New images appeared in my brain. Brandy would be next on my interview list.

Penelope Farquhar sat beside her, wearing the female version of a Harrington jacket with a t-shirt, dark skirt and low-heeled shoes, the trendy/professional look. I understood her wish to be admired for her writing. How far would she go to protect her point of view?

After Psalms, prayers, and a reading from the Gospel, the Reverend McClintock began his homily. For the first time, he spoke the name of Kermit Carmody, and the deceased became part of the service. He recalled Kermit's childhood with his parents and brother, and then went straight to the professor's academic achievements. He prayed for Carmody, the mourners and the Christian community and tossed the ball to Eric Lager.

When Eric walked to the front, I noticed his pants rose three inches off the floor. Highwaters. For his boss's funeral. I understood he preferred studying cells and enzymes, but couldn't he glance in a mirror to see if his pants approached the vicinity of his shoes?

He stepped onto the platform wearing a gray threadbare suit that matched his hair and a string tie. He looked like the undertaker in an old Texas movie. He reached in his pocket for notecards, placed them on the podium and cleared his throat.

"I know we're all saddened by Dr. Carmody's sudden death. But he would want us to carry on. Learning and research were his life." As he mouthed "research," his gaze involuntarily landed on me. A few students I recognized sliced eyes toward me. They'd read my column. Penelope leaned forward, peered down the pew and gave me a disdainful glance as though she was quite familiar with every plebeian word I'd written.

Eric Lager praised Carmody and listed his accomplishments and discoveries, occasionally nodding to scientists who had apparently worked with him.

"To show how far we've come in the past ten years," Eric intoned, "when Dr. Carmody and I attended NIH's conference in April, scientists agreed that cystic fibrosis was a well-characterized, serious genetic disease inherited from a genetic disorder mapped to chromosome 7. They believed isolating the gene could lead to curative gene therapy and ultimately, prevention of the disease." He smiled proudly. Maybe he was demonstrating how close he and Carmody were, close enough so that *he* would now assume the premier scientific mantle.

He offered no intimate or humorous recollections of his former colleague. He might as well have handed out the professor's *curriculum vitae* with bibliography attached.

"There will be a reception for Dr. Carmody here in the parish hall after the service." He emerged from behind the podium and walked down the steps.

No family members rose to eulogize the professor. Had Dr. Carmody been more preoccupied with cells in laboratories than cells created into human beings?

Father McClintock said final prayers and committed Dr. Carmody to eternal rest—a less-than-idyllic prospect, I thought, for a man whose eagerness for discovery far outweighed his desire to rest. The final hymn was "All Things Bright and Beautiful," which I found incongruous for a man who, so far as I knew, rarely found things bright or beautiful outside the laboratory.

Then I remembered that tiny moment when he'd said, "I'll try to live up to your perception of what I can do." He must have had other such moments. I was proud to have been present for a rare glimpse into who he really was. He'd dedicated his life to improving humanity. Tragically, he might have taken the knowledge prematurely to his grave.

Penelope had found somebody to flirt with. I stepped into the aisle and waited for her. As fellow writers, surely we could have some sort of camaraderie.

"Go on ahead," I told Meredith. "I'm going to chat with Penelope. Want to drop in briefly at the reception?"

"Sure. I'll try to learn how long Carmody had been ill."

As I lingered, Eric Lager sidled up. "I read your column. A nice tribute to Dr. Carmody. You seem quite interested in his work."

"I am. I'd love to see his workplace."

"Your class will eventually visit the lab. It's on the schedule. But I guess I could give you a quick preliminary tour."

"Do you think it's appropriate?"

"I think he'd be pleased."

"I suppose I could." I was dying to learn what Carmody had been working on. To figure out what might have killed him, I'd have to visit both the lab and his home.

"I don't know how long people will stay at the reception," he said. "Why don't you come over to the lab around five?"

"That will work. I'll see you then."

He turned and joined the exodus leaving the church. Penelope finally made her way to the aisle.

"Nice service," I said.

"Yes. Too bad he died, though. Especially for those of us interested in his work."

She turned heel. It appeared Penelope and I were not going to become friends.

As I passed through the church doors, I saw Sam standing off to one side, scrutinizing the exiting mourners. He'd probably studied photos and bios of UHT's faculty and scientists who worked in Carmody's field and might attend his funeral. He must share my suspicion that Carmody's death wasn't accidental. Otherwise, why study the attendees? Sam's name was apparently not on the guest list for the morning memorial service. UHT wouldn't be eager to have police officers there until they had some idea of what had happened to their star professor. Sam wouldn't press the issue, but he'd probably already obtained a list of students, faculty and guests.

I felt guilty watching him screw up his face trying to recall specifics about each person. I should go back inside the church and ask forgiveness for my omission and tell Sam everything. But I viewed my interviews with possible suspects as an attempt to achieve justice and help Sam. I simply wasn't quite ready to discuss my plans with him.

I walked with him to the parish hall, making small talk about the service.

"What did you learn at the memorial this morning?" he asked.

"That several people had reason to dislike Dr. Carmody. I'll write their names down for you later." I walked faster, entered the parish hall and headed for Dr. Carmody's brother in the receiving line.

"It was a lovely service," I said. "I'm so sorry for your loss."

"Thank you both for coming." Claude shook our hands without giving me a chance to introduce Sam. "I'll get some investment information together for you," he said, looking toward the next person in line.

I knew Sam would head for the food table, so I slipped away to survey the room. Not seeing any people I knew were scientists, or Meredith, I left the parish hall, walked back past the entrance to the church and descended the steps toward her car. She was seated when I hopped in. I didn't mention my appointment with Eric Lager.

"Did you learn anything at the reception?" I asked.

"Only that I'm ready to go home."

Seventeen

At soon as she dropped me at home, I changed from funeral attire into slacks and a blouse. It was three p.m., and I wasn't due at the lab until five. I entered Carmody's phone number into the reverse directory and found his address. I hopped into Albatross, steered down Burr Road and turned south on Broadway.

People at St. Peter's would still be visiting or heading for home. With the results of Carmody's autopsy unknown, police wouldn't be scouring his apartment. It was the perfect time to snoop. Since I thought he'd been murdered, this was my best chance to find a link to his killer and a clue to the motive.

I'd heard that Carmody and other UHT staff members lived in apartment buildings south of the university off Broadway, the main thoroughfare between the lush campus setting of Uptown Broadway and the downtown area leading to the tourist-filled San Antonio River Walk.

A few blocks south of Hildebrand, I veered left off Broadway onto a side street. About a block down, a gray-painted brick apartment complex abutted land at the west side of Ft. Sam Houston. The two-story apartments probably stayed full because of their proximity to the post. Neat and tidy, they lay in a large two-story U around a center grassy area. I estimated there were sixty to seventy-five apartments. There wasn't much shade in the center area, but the right leg of the U was shadowed by trees. It would be easy for me to wander there unobserved. Carmody's apartment number indicated he was on the ground floor, so I casually meandered toward the tree-canopied area. If anyone asked, I'd say I was interested in renting a unit.

I rummaged in my handbag for the discarded dental pick I secured from my dentist. It worked pretty well on most locks. I wasn't accustomed to picking locks, but I liked to be prepared. When I was sure no one was around, I found Carmody's apartment and slid the implement into the lock. It clicked. I slipped inside, eased the door closed and reminded myself not to touch anything.

His living room looked like the aftermath of a tornado. Except for his television and swivel chair, nothing looked strategically placed. Desks with chairs sat randomly around the room. Papers covered the desks and some had fallen to the floor. The air conditioner was still on, but the apartment smelled stale, as though the windows had never been opened. I peered into the kitchen. Dirty dishes filled the sink with old teabags staining the porcelain. In the bedroom, the bed lay unmade—no surprise there. A bottle of his nasal spray sat on the nightstand. No photographs personalized the room. Not one. No wonder he wasn't department chair. He didn't seem to have any relationships, and he was way too messy.

I peeked into the bathroom, grabbed some tissue to wrap my fingers and opened the medicine cabinet. I found aspirin, Tylenol, and Propanalol, the drug to reduce high blood pressure. Brother Claude hadn't mentioned Kermit's blood pressure. Some people were highly allergic to Propanalol. Carmody had raved about the drug in his diatribe. People with high blood pressure were more prone to have strokes and heart attacks.

I heard steps outside the building. It was after four p.m. People must be coming home from work. I perused the living room, wishing I had time to start the desktop computer and search Carmody's files. The best I could do was skirt between desks looking for papers with familiar words. I knew that if Carmody was murdered and I snitched something, I'd be guilty of tampering with evidence, in addition to breaking and entering,

One paper referred to "daf-2." I grabbed it. I read "telomerase" on another paper and swooped it up. Folding the sheets carefully, I slipped them into my purse and tiptoed behind the front door to listen. My heart was about to beat through my blouse. I hadn't touched a thing, except for the papers I took.

People conversed outside. When I heard another door open and the sound of voices receding into an apartment, I peered around the door. Seeing no one, I slipped through, closed it silently behind me, left the complex and walked briskly to my car.

The inside of Albatross felt like an oven. I locked the doors, started the car, clicked on the AC and swept my gaze around the area. Apparently, no one had seen me. Taking a series of deep breaths, I eased onto Broadway and drove north toward the UHT campus.

Eighteen

At a little past five p.m., it was still sweltering. The days were getting shorter, but the parched land thirsted for rain and relief from the sun. I parked on a side street in the shade of the science building, entered the building and walked down the hall, thankful for the invention of air conditioning. Professor Eric Lager held the door to the lab open.

"I'm glad you made it. The reception is over, and everybody is finally headed home. I'm drinking V8 juice to get my veggies and carry me until suppertime. Care for some?"

The cold, healthy drink sounded good. He handed me V8 over ice and I sipped. "Hmm. Salt tastes good. This heat really dehydrates you."

"Yes. I should probably buy the low-sodium variety. Welcome to our cell genetics teaching lab."

"Thank you. Did you enjoy the reception?" I hadn't seen him there.

He shrugged. "It was okay. The scientists all tried to impress each other and pump me about projects Carmody and I were working on."

"His death was so unexpected. I can see why they're curious. You must have found it fascinating to work alongside him."

"He was autocratic, but brilliant. Our work was important."

No personal regret. Only the work. Eric Lager was a cold fish.

The lab was larger than I expected, with counters around the periphery and sinks installed at intervals. Supply boxes, gloves, rubber tubing and black boxes as big as microwaves covered counters. The room had a medicinal odor I couldn't identify. Probably some cleaning compound. Countertops indented at various intervals allowed chairs to slip underneath to create workspaces. A computer sat at one workspace, perhaps where Dr. Carmody or his assistants entered data. I wondered if this computer communicated with the one at his apartment.

Windows flanked the far side of the lab, but the shades were drawn against the heat. Cabinets on sidewalls held glass vials, plastic bottles and glass tubes. There was space in the center of the room for freestanding counters with drawers and room for round pedestal tables surrounded by rolling chairs.

"We're fortunate to have this space," he said. "Once we signed on to be part of the genome project, we received a huge grant and were able to expand the lab and equip it comparably to labs in large research universities." He pointed to a table. "We recently got those 1000X stereo microscopes."

"Can you see the *C. elegans* roundworm with those?"

"Yes."

"I remember you saying how you separate DNA into strands using chemicals or electricity."

"We can break DNA into single strands using that electrophoresis chamber." He pointed to a clear plastic rectangular box sitting on a freestanding cabinet. "We plug power cables into the chamber and use two thousand volts to separate the strands. But if the electric current gets too hot, the gel around the DNA melts. And if somebody puts both hands in the gel buffer inside the chamber, they get a nasty shock. There's a safety lid on the machine, but some people don't bother with it. Plus, we have to stain the gel with ethidium bromide, which is considered a carcinogen in powder form. You have to wear a mask and gloves when handling it. We still have stock of the old powder that nobody threw away." He pointed up to a high shelf with containers labeled "Ethidium Bromide."

"Don't you worry that somebody could inhale the powder?"

"Nobody gets those containers down. And the powder is a bright reddish-purple color...hard to miss. It's a rarely used procedure. Now we use enzymes to cut entire genes out of the genome."

He was pretty casual about dangers in the lab. Who else knew about the powder? Did somebody manage to have Carmody unknowingly inhale the chemical?

I didn't reveal my suspicions that Dr. Carmody had been murdered. Eric Lager would clam up. He was a fountain of information. He could also be a prime suspect.

"After you use enzymes to cut genes out of the genome, what do you do next?"

"Using original genes and genes we've copied, we insert some into a bacteria which produces a blue color. We do all this in a sterile environment. Follow me. I'll show you."

He opened the door to a smaller room. Long and narrow, the space looked like an oversized storage closet. I noted that the door at the far end of the room opened into the main hall, parallel to the main door we used to enter the lab.

He walked to a piece of equipment with a waist-high perforated metal tray and extended his forearms over the tray.

"We work with our genes, enzymes and bacteria here." A clear hood floated above his arms. "Ultraviolet light from the culture hood over my hands illuminates the work area and keeps it sterile."

"Can't ultraviolet light damage your cells?"

"If a person is under UV light too long or looks directly at the light, his cells will suffer damage. UV light also increases progerin. All humans have some progerin, but if we have a genetic mutation which allows too much of the toxic protein to be produced, we'll get the disease progeria. Since you write an anti-aging column, you're probably familiar with progeria."

"Where children degenerate into old age and die young?"

"Yes. We know a genetic mutation causes the condition, but we don't know yet why the gene mutates. We do know that UV rays increase progerin. You probably shouldn't get too close."

Was he just hassling me, or was the danger real? I stepped back from the hooded tray, eager to change the subject.

"So you're preparing to see how some agent will change individual genes?"

"Yes. We put genes mixed with culture mediums on agar plates and into the cellular incubator."

He strode back into the lab, stopped just beyond the door and pointed to a machine that looked like a mini-refrigerator. "That's the 37°C incubator. Cells stored inside reproduce at human body temperature."

His fish grin gave me the creeps. I wanted to obtain as much information as possible and leave.

"I guess you and Dr. Carmody were adding the enzyme telomerase to various types of cells to see what effect it had? Whether it prolonged the life of the cells? Or whether some other substance you added would inactivate telomerase so the cells died?"

He studied me with a look of appraisal. "That was one of our interests. Researchers try to make progress until they hit a dead end, or before a scientist using another approach makes a breakthrough."

Or until a scientist makes a discovery and is murdered by a jealous competitor?

"I'm sure you can appreciate the pressure of time passing too fast," he said, "since you're concerned with aging." He attempted to smile.

He obviously enjoyed needling me. Working with a grumpy autocrat like Dr. Carmody who probably didn't appreciate him must have been frustrating. Was he discouraged, wondering if his own chances for scientific renown were slipping away under the tutelage of the famous Dr. Kermit Carmody?

"Did you also add substances to the APOE proteins they think might affect the onset of Alzheimer's?"

His eyes became slits. "That was another of our interests."

It appeared I wasn't going to extract more information from Eric Lager.

"I know he was interested in the daf-2 gene and in telomeres. He dropped some papers about them before our first class. I picked them up and have been meaning to give them to Dr. Bigsby. She's expecting them." I smiled.

He glowered at me with eyes that were no longer friendly. It was time to leave, but I had to ask one more question.

"Had Dr. Carmody been ill for a long time?"

"He had horrible allergies that sapped his strength. Other than that..." He shrugged and stretched his fish mouth into a thin line.

"I'd better go," I said. "I've enjoyed this so much, I didn't notice it was getting late." Light had disappeared from behind the drawn window shades. I headed for the door. He reached the door first and held the knob secure as he peered down at me.

"It's encouraging to see a student so interested in scientific discovery." One side of his mouth curled.

"Yes. For my column."

"Of course." He nodded and released the doorknob. I scooted through the door, down the hall and out of the building into suffocating heat, forced to take deep breaths to slow my heartbeat. Now I knew why Eric Lager had invited me to tour the lab. He intended to scare me from ever coming back.

Dusk had descended into darkness. Campus lights glowed softly. People crossed through light circles and shadows walking to their cars.

I spotted Brandy strolling with another scientist I'd seen flirting with her at the funeral. It wasn't Stanley or Phillip. They walked side by side, smiling at each other.

When they stopped by a tree with their faces close together, it looked like they kissed, but it was too dark for me to be sure. I glanced up at the backlit clock tower. Rising from darkness over the shadowy campus, the pinnacle of hope appeared ominous.

The spot where I'd parked Albatross, overshadowed by the gloomy hulk of the science building, was pitch dark. I walked on hot pavement to the driver's side, probing for my keys. As my hand closed around them, I heard a noise and a swish and felt an excruciating blow to the back of my head. I lunged for the door handle and slumped to the asphalt.

Nineteen

Car lights hit my face. I blinked my eyes open in time to roll halfway under my car, over my keys. After the car passed, I swiveled back toward fresh air, trembling. My head pounded and my stomach reeled. I rolled out onto the pavement. On hands and knees, I fumbled for my keys. Clutching them, I crawled on hot asphalt around the back of my car. I made it to the curb and threw up on the grass. Panting, I tried to regain the strength to stand. After I wiped my mouth, I groped for the purse strap still on my shoulder. Feeling down the strap, I unzipped the purse, dropped the car keys inside and fumbled for a tissue. I felt my wallet with money and credit cards. Carmody's papers were gone.

I searched the darkness, my head throbbing. Seeing no one, I grabbed hold of Albatross's bumper, pulled myself up and tugged my body around the car to the driver's side. The moon glowed white on paper trapped beneath my windshield wipers. Carmody's papers? I reached for them, opened the door and threw them inside. Collapsing into the seat, I locked the doors. Struggling to breathe the hot stale air, I started the engine and turned on the AC. Tilting the paper toward moonlight, I realized it didn't belong to Carmody. I blinked at blocked, crude letters scratched on a single sheet, "You're not wanted here. Take this warning. STAY AWAY."

Despite feeling nauseous, I managed to drive home. With relief, I drove into my garage, slipped through the door to the kitchen and locked myself inside. After heading to the bathroom to splash my face and brush my teeth, I grabbed a hand mirror to view the back of my head in the mirror above the sink. Caked blood splayed my hair, and a mound swelled underneath. Fearful of washing my head, I sponged blood off with a damp towel. The bump lay behind the crown of my head. The spot didn't hurt unless I touched it, and I thought I could rearrange my thick hair to camouflage it. It was high enough that I should be able to sleep without putting pressure on the lump.

The attack could have been much worse. But somebody was desperate to keep me from gaining further knowledge about Carmody's research. The most obvious person and the one closest to the attack was Eric Lager, but scads of people were leaving campus after Carmody's reception, including Brandy Crystal and her boyfriend. Any one of Dr. Carmody's disgruntled colleagues could have seen me enter or exit the lab, followed me, hit me, found the papers in my purse and deposited their crude warning.

My column had more effect than I intended. I expected Carmody's fellow scientists to squabble among themselves, expose their deadly jealousies and take some sort of action which would point to the one who wanted him dead. I never expected anyone to come after me.

The magnitude of Dr. Carmody's death was sinking in. It might take years before anybody learned how to alter genes to delay aging. My chances of staying young and attractive were looking dim. My chances for staying alive weren't looking too good either.

If I lived long enough to gather the courage to reveal my secret to Sam, I'd probably be too old for him to love me. I pictured my dismal future: withering youth, no job and no Sam. If only he were here to comfort me.

My phone rang.

"Aggie, you sure were in a hurry after Carmody's funeral. I tried to catch you, but you and Meredith drove off too fast."

I closed my eyes and sighed, relishing the sound of his voice. I imagined his arms wrapped around me.

"I had errands to run," I told him, "and I stumbled off a curb on the way home and hit my head."

"Is it bad? Should I come over?"

Should I let him come? Could I shower and change clothes without bumping my head? Could he kiss me without hurting my head? He must have heard me sigh.

"Why don't I bring some soup? And some wine, if you feel like having company. I was up most of last night on a tough case. It's been a long day. I won't stay late."

Even smiling made my head throb. "I have tons of salad to go with the soup."

Twenty

I managed to shower and dress without hitting my bump and used my dryer to fluff hair up around the protrusion. The mound looked strange, but it felt protective.

After I sprayed perfume on my hair, I popped the White Stones' *Secret Garden* into my stereo, soothing music I didn't think would make my head throb. When the doorbell rang, I had just released some produce from the refrigerator. So much greenery looked revolting. Right now, I'd just as soon eat grass.

When I opened the door, Sam stood there in khakis, holding a grocery bag. He grinned.

"I brought two cartons of deli soup, crackers and two bottles of wine." He followed me to the kitchen, put things down and took me in his arms. "I'm sorry about your head. Want to show me?"

"No. It's okay." Everything was okay. I just didn't want him to start thinking about how I managed to trip off a curb and land on the crown of my head. He took my face in his hands and kissed me. He looked into my eyes, smiled and kissed me again. Then he drew me close and held me tighter. His breathing changed.

I pulled gently away and kissed his cheek. "My head's pounding a little. Do you think it's all right to take two Advil with a glass of wine?"

"I don't think it'll hurt." He handed me the bottle of capsules and went to open the wine while I swallowed two pills with a handful of tap water. I rinsed salad greens, sliced tomatoes and baby spinach and put them into a colander to drain.

"What did you think of Dr. Carmody's funeral?" I asked.

"The service was pretty impersonal."

"That's what I thought. Surely someone had fond memories of the man." I lifted my two best placemats from a drawer, grabbed napkins and utensils and arranged them on the square wood coffee table between my sofas. When I bent to place the settings side by side so we could sit on the same sofa, my head throbbed and I felt dizzy. I should probably have had my head x-rayed, but once Sam called...

"Did you notice the two women sitting at the left end of my pew?" I said. "Brandy Crystal and Penelope Farquhar. Men kept turning to eyeball them. Penelope writes for AARP, and Brandy is Eric Lager's lab assistant. They're both in my class."

"I did see them. I should find out who they were flirting with. The men could be scientists who made visits to Carmody's lab."

"They might know what he was working on." If I'd known the name of the man strolling with Brandy, I would have told him. But I'd have to explain why I was traipsing around campus after dark.

"Which woman was Dr. Bigsby?" he asked.

I hated to describe her as Popeye's girlfriend Olive Oyl. "Well, she's tall, but she doesn't stand out because she wears subdued clothes, her hair in a bun..."

"Right. I saw her."

I tossed the salad with sugar-free, fat-free dressing that I hoped wouldn't make him gag. Even the tossing movement made my head hurt. We heated our soups in the microwave and made our way to the sofa. Sam brought the wine and glasses.

I lowered myself gingerly onto the sofa, holding my head steady.

"You should be checked out after that fall. Tell me again how that happened."

"Just a silly misstep. I'm fine." I held up my glass. "Cheers." The wine tasted good. Besides having a headache, I felt weak.

Sam plunged into eating. I tasted the soup, and my stomach flipped. When I put down the spoon, he looked over.

"The soup is delicious, but I'm not too hungry. I'll save it for later. You go ahead."

While he polished off his meal, I sat very still and willed my stomach to settle. By the time he finished eating and smiled at me, I felt better but different, like a rag doll with a porcelain head. I felt secure with him sitting beside me on my sofa. We were teammates. Soulmates. I smiled at him. "Have you ever thought of opening a private investigation firm when you retire?"

He laughed. "I will have spent more than enough time solving crimes." He put his arm around me, moved closer and kissed me. "Feeling better?"

"Hmmm."

He kissed me on my forehead. Overcome by the urge to snuggle, I rested the side of my head on his shoulder, cuddled into him like a child and closed my eyes.

"You may have a concussion that's making you sleepy."

"Hmmm."

"I'll stay for a while so I can wake you if you go to sleep."

"Hmmm."

When I woke, my head felt like a basketball on a spring. Sam lay stretched lengthwise on the sofa, snoring, with his feet sticking toward me. What would it be like, after busy days and delicious nights, to wake up and see him lying next to me, relaxed and peaceful?

I stretched my stiff neck toward the window, saw daylight and checked my watch: six a.m. His all-nighter the night before last had taken its toll.

While he snored, I considered telling him what I'd done and everything that had happened. But I knew he'd be furious. If I wanted him to appreciate me as an investigator and view me with respect as an equal, I had to take a few risks. My head would be okay. I'd come a long way toward flushing out Carmody's killer. If I succeeded in exposing the person who killed the renowned Dr.

Carmody, my self-esteem would skyrocket, and Sam would take notice. I wanted to be more than just his old, comfortable friend.

Rising as quietly as I could, I sneaked to the back of my cottage to dress, closing the door to my bedroom so the noise wouldn't wake him. I planned to eat breakfast at Wendy's and let him sleep. When I was dressed and ready to leave, I tiptoed back to the living room and covered him with a blanket. Leaving a note on the table, I slid through the kitchen door into the garage.

Twenty-One

Fortified by my Wendy's breakfast, I decided to interview Brandy Crystal. UHT had apartments at one end of campus for graduate students and visiting professors. I'd heard the apartments were pretty plush compared to other campus housing. Maybe the man she'd kissed under the tree lived in one of the units.

I'd entered her phone number from Carmody's list into the reverse directory and found her address: Garden Apartment Q, UHT. Stanley Bly lived in Apartment B.

After driving around campus, I located the Garden Apartments and snagged a parking spot. The five-story brick building, built around an open enclosure, looked newer than others on campus. In a breezeway at ground level, I found Brandy's name listed for Apartment Q and took the elevator to the top.

I stepped off into a courtyard with a large hot tub in the center surrounded by lawn tables and chairs shaded by umbrellas. Plush. Across the corners of the building, apartments were separated by head-high trellises partially covered with flowering vines. The sweet smell of honeysuckle was intoxicating. I squinted. Were those clothes blowing on a line behind the corner trellis? What a clever way to hang laundry in fresh air. Or you could bask in your own private patio.

To the right of each apartment entry door, five-foot high trellises ran the width of each unit. The delicate odor permeating the patio smelled like paradise. UHT must have paid a clever architect a substantial sum for the design.

I thought I saw Brandy enter her trellised nook from inside Apartment Q. I walked over and peeped through the latticework.

"Brandy, is that you?"

She jumped.

"It's Aggie Mundeen from Science of Aging."

"Oh." She sounded disappointed. "Come to the front. I'll let you in." Shola Ama's "You Might Need Somebody" blared from her apartment. When she opened the door, I thought she was expecting somebody, but not me.

Fuchsia pink hoops piercing her earlobes matched the neon pink camisole stretched across her braless chest. Her silky green shorts clung like glue. She must work out a lot to have such a perfect figure. I could exercise until I collapsed and never look like that. Her dark eyes were lined in musky brown framed by mascara-clad lashes. Her hair was spiked to perfection. She was barefoot.

"I was expecting..." She checked her Timex. "It's only nine o'clock. Come on in."

A streamlined apple green sofa, two flower-patterned chairs and glass tables floated on the faux wood-planked floor. She skimmed across the surface on tiny feet. Despite my new jeans and crisp t-shirt, I felt like a clumsy oaf swaddled in burlap.

A picture window banked the entire outside wall across from the door. The wide sill held a funky teapot and green shoots in slender glass containers. Some of the plants were ivy; others looked like they'd spent their formative years in a laboratory and were struggling to develop into plants.

"Have a seat. Want herbal tea?" She gyrated to the radio and decreased the volume.

"No thanks. I saw you at Dr. Carmody's funeral and thought I'd come over and commiserate. Can you believe he's actually gone?"

"No. He's been part of my life for so long. Ever since freshman biology at Boston University."

"If I remember correctly, you were also a graduate and doctoral student there?"

"That's right." She blinked heavy lashes. Did her eyes grow moist, or did I imagine it?

"I remember you said you loved Boston. Did you consider staying there to teach?"

The corners of her mouth drooped. "It's difficult for a woman to succeed if she stays at the institution where she trains. She becomes a fixture—one of the in-house females. The department is always searching for the star scientist, the white knight they recruit from outside to elevate their program."

She pinched her mouth into a pout and gazed toward the window, where flat-bottomed glass vials on the ledge held an array of decorative powdery sands.

Their color ranged from white to yellow to pink to purple to reddish-purple.

"Those sands are lovely," I said, walking toward the sill.

"I enjoy experimenting with colors."

"Are they powders? Sand?"

"Some of both." She walked back toward the sofa.

I wished I could snitch a couple of vials to take to a private laboratory for analysis, especially the one with the reddish-purple powder that matched Eric Lager's description of ethidium bromide. The chemical could have decomposed over time and be harmless. But why did Brandy have it?

There was no way I could grab the vials. I followed her to the sofa and sat.

"Did you do research in Boston?"

"Yes. I was sought after as a researcher by Carmody and others. He was young and promising. It was fun. Sometimes I was head collaborator on research papers, first author, sometimes second author. There might be a dozen collaborators listed. It's understood that ideas generated by coworkers are considered the professor's ideas, so Professor Carmody's name always appeared at the honored place on articles. No matter how many people collaborated, others said that 'Carmody discovered' or 'Carmody and coworkers discovered,' and they ignored all the other names."

"Yet you had a doctorate and were obviously capable."

"Other professors gave more credit. They said things like 'Here are the names of the people who did all the work' or 'My role was minimal, I just stood out of Smith's way.' They were being modest, of course, maybe falsely modest. But Dr. Carmody never bothered to share credit. I got tired of being relegated to 'et al' or 'coworker' status." She folded her arms.

I knew the difficulty of succeeding as a woman from climbing the corporate ladder of my Chicago bank. Banks were relatively open to female advancement, yet I had to work harder and smarter to make it to vice president. I'd heard that in academia, women were prominent in research and lauded accordingly.

Had the academic society embittered this young woman? Had she given up marriage and family to climb the academic ladder, only to be knocked to the bottom too many times?

"If you felt ignored in Dr. Carmody's Boston lab, why did you follow him here?"

She shrugged. "He has great ideas."

"You assisted Dr. Carmody with groundbreaking research?"

"Yes."

"Were you as fascinated as he was by the prospects of manipulating telomeres?"

"Yes." She smiled at the irresistible power of discovery.

"And learning the daf-2 gene could 'power' downstream genes to make changes that might affect aging?" I was getting excited. We were grinning at each other. "Did you work with him on APOE genes related to Alzheimer's disease?"

She squinted at me. Her smile faded into a noncommittal expression. "We worked on a lot of projects."

It appeared Brandy was done sharing information. "Working by Dr. Carmody's side for so long must be a great comfort to you."

She checked her watch.

"I'd better go. I'm glad you're doing okay." That was an understatement. She was drop-dead gorgeous. And grief hadn't subdued her taste in clothes. "I'll see you in class tomorrow."

"Sure. Nice to see you." She hustled me out and closed the door.

I walked to the corner elevator and pushed the button. When the door opened, Sam stood there.

Twenty-Two

His eyes widened. "I didn't expect to see you here."

I pictured Brandy's stretched camisole. *I bet you didn't.* I hiked my chin. "I thought I'd visit some of my classmates."

"Remember I told you I'd talk to Brandy about scientists who visited Carmody?"

"Sure." He'd have a hard time thinking about Carmody once he laid eyes on that hot pink. It was ridiculous to be jealous because Sam interviewed a dead man's colleague. He was doing his job. But her figure was perfect. Dressed like she was, she was obviously expecting somebody special. She wasn't shy. And she was probably fifteen years younger than me.

I marched around Sam and stomped into the elevator.

"Wait, Aggie. Are you feeling better? I guess you are. I need to talk to you, as soon as I finish with...finish interviewing Brandy."

I pushed the button. As the door rolled to close, I scorched him with a penetrating look. "It shouldn't take you long."

As the door shut, he stood there with his mouth hanging open.

I descended to the ground floor with angry steam rising off me, probably making the elevator hotter. When the door opened, I puffed and tromped to the car.

Okay, I was jealous. She was young, gorgeous and smart, and she'd been expecting him. All dolled up. Did she dress that way for every man? She could shimmy out of that camisole like a molting snake. If that was her usual *modus operandi*, Dr. Carmody wouldn't have stood a chance. He probably died from a heart attack just thinking about her. Maybe they'd had practice sessions. Maybe when they started, he was virile and young and her ticket to fame. Did she figure it was worth sleeping with the old coot to share his discoveries? How long had that been going on? Now that he'd croaked on her, what would she do?

She'd have to work out new angles. Professor Eric Lager was an intriguing, if revolting, possibility. The scientist she'd been cozy with under the stars might be a target. The two postdocs might be in the running. Was she buttering up men capable of helping her confiscate Carmody's work? Were any of them murder suspects?

And there was Sam. He could be her insurance policy in case she needed to use law enforcement to lay claim to Carmody's discoveries. She might be ripening him up, along with her other prospects. That thought made me nauseous.

But maybe I was wrong about Brandy. Her flirtatious demeanor and skimpy clothes were hard to ignore, but maybe that was just who she was.

Sam said he needed to talk to me. If I could find someplace where we wouldn't get heatstroke, maybe I should see what he had to say.

I spotted a bench under a shade tree that faced the ground floor of the building. From there, I could see Sam when he came off the elevator. It was nine forty-five a.m. I would also know how long he stayed upstairs with Brandy.

Thirty minutes seemed like an eternity until he emerged from the elevator at ten fifteen. He looked pretty normal ambling toward his car until he saw me. His face lit up.

"I didn't know if you'd stay. I'm glad you did. How's your head? I was afraid to leave you last night in case you had a concussion, but I fell asleep...I'm an idiot. Your note said you'd get breakfast but you didn't say where. Are you okay?"

Bless his heart. He'd been concerned about me last night and was concerned about me now. Brandy couldn't make him feel that way. At least not yet. Maybe she was just a young girl who enjoyed showing off her assets.

"My head still hurts, but I think it'll be okay. Did you learn anything about the scientists who came to see Carmody?"

"Not really. She said he might have kept a list of their names in the lab. She was pretty closed-mouthed. Mostly she wanted to flirt. Which was *not* why I was there."

I smiled. "There was something you wanted to tell me?"

"I read the medical examiner's autopsy report. Carmody didn't die of a stroke or heart attack. He died of a fungal infection."

"A fungus? How in the world..."

"It apparently started in his head. His nasal passages and brain were inflamed. The ME called it fungal meningitis. From his brain, the fungus spread through his body. It was too massive for his immune system to fight it off."

"Wouldn't antibiotics help?"

"Antibiotics apparently have no effect on a fungus."

"His nasal passages...he had allergies and was always spraying Afrin up his nose."

"We need to get our hands on that bottle. The fungus could have been in it."

"You think he got a bad batch of nasal spray?" I remembered the spray bottle I'd seen by Carmody's bed. I couldn't go back. SAPD was probably en route to his apartment. They would find it. "Could somebody have put fungus in his Afrin bottle? To kill him?"

"That's what the ME thinks happened. Somebody grew the fungus and planted it in the Afrin, knowing he'd spray it up his nose. With everyone assuming he had a stroke or heart attack, and EMS attempting to revive him, no one paid attention to the nose spray. As soon as I talked to the ME, I went to the classroom to look for it. Not surprisingly, it wasn't there. But we're treating this like a homicide, which means you can't talk to any more classmates. We'll talk to the president of UHT. He'll probably want to keep Carmody's cause of death quiet. Everybody's a suspect, and we'll interview them discreetly. You should probably drop the class."

"I can't possibly do that. I'm sure classes will continue as usual. They'll try to maintain a normal class schedule."

"That's probably true. But, Aggie..."

I looked up with raised brows.

"You could be in close proximity to a killer."

If only he knew how close. I shivered remembering Penelope's apparent determination to discredit Dr. Carmody's approach, the lab tour, my head bashing, and the suspicious colored powders on Brandy's window sill. I should tell him all this, but I was getting close enough to actually solve this crime myself. I could put the pieces together and then tell him everything.

"You should go straight to class and leave as soon as it's over. Don't engage anyone in class or any scientists on campus. You can tell Meredith what killed Carmody, but have her keep it confidential. I read your column suggesting the direction of Carmody's research. Don't write any more provocative articles about him or about what he might have been doing."

"You don't have to raise your voice." I knew he cared about me and was trying to protect me. What he didn't know was that a major motivation for my even taking the class was to stay young and interesting for him. I was glad he didn't know I'd conducted other interviews and received an enlightening tour of the lab. That would really set him off.

He was right to think we were dealing with a desperate person who would do anything to keep me or anybody else from knowing the details of Carmody's work. That person probably killed Carmody and whapped me on the head.

My study of anti-aging was getting way too personal. I could expend all my energy to stay young and vital and end up dead.

He put me in my car, admonished me again, told me to report anything suspicious around my house and said he was going to headquarters to check the backgrounds of every scientist within a thousand-mile radius who worked in Carmody's field.

"You might consider interviewing Eric Lager," I said, turning on the ignition. "Even though he's not as young and cute as his assistant." I couldn't resist saying it. Looking straight ahead, I pulled Albatross away from the curb and lurched forward.

Twenty-Three

I knew I'd have to return to Dr. Carmody's lab. His computer was there. I might find his research notes in a drawer and the list of scientists he worked with. Even students' notes could be helpful. I'd studied the lab pretty carefully, but if Carmody's killer left a clue, something regarding the deadly fungus might catch my eye. I'd have to be very careful.

If Eric killed Carmody, he probably scrubbed the place clean before he gave me the tour. But how would I know whether he changed anything after I left except to go back there?

UHT would make every effort to have the university operate as usual. The science building would have to remain open for classes. If it was locked, I thought I could open the building and the lab door with my dental implement.

I couldn't break into Carmody's apartment again. SAPD would be swarming it. They'd test his nasal spray and the drugs in his bathroom and try to make sense of his scientific papers. They'd search for fingerprints. Hopefully mine wouldn't be there.

If I told Sam everything, it meant confessing to touring the lab with suspect Eric Lager, getting whacked on the head instead of stumbling off a curb, receiving a warning note from a probable killer and interviewing Penelope Farquhar and Hortense Bigsby, in addition to Brandy with the stretched-out Spandex.

I'd been trying to summon courage to tell Sam the secret from my past that I feared would doom our relationship. Confessing more lies and omissions now would not further my cause. He'd be furious. If I could just help him solve this crime, he might find me brave and intriguing, and we could take it from there.

But I had a problem: my head still hurt. At times, I felt dizzy. I wasn't sure I should even be driving. Meredith had mentioned her family doctor, a specialist in internal medicine. Maybe she could get me in to see him.

When I got home, I called her. She got me an emergency appointment and picked me up. I told her Carmody didn't die of a heart attack and was killed by a fungus in his nasal spray. It felt wonderful spilling at least part of the beans.

We arrived at her internist's office in the Medical Sky office building. After Dr. Satcher asked me a slew of general questions, he sent us to the radiologist down the hall. Dr. Knowles' nurse instructed me to swath myself in a sheet. After he asked me more questions, they took me to a room and had me recline like a mummy with my head stuck in an MRI tube. The noisy apparatus made my headache worse. When the MRI was finally over and I was dressing, I heard familiar voices in the hall.

"It's better if she doesn't know you're here," Meredith said, "but I had to call you. I'm concerned."

"Okay, we won't mention it," Sam said.

I couldn't believe she'd called him.

"Falling off that curb could be serious. Then when she told me Carmody was probably murdered, I had to call you."

Thank goodness I hadn't told Meredith about my interviews and lab tour.

"Has she seemed touchy to you lately, a little grouchy?" he asked.

Spandex tugged across a girl's boobs for every man to ogle tends to make other women grouchy.

"She's been acting a little different," Meredith said.

Criminal investigations make you tense. I couldn't tell her everything I'd been doing. Obviously. Blabbermouth.

"This class means so much to her," she said. "She's always been interested in how to stop aging, and geneticists are now probing the secrets. Dr. Carmody wasn't her favorite professor, but she felt sorry for him. She sensed right from the start he didn't die from a stroke or heart attack. She's determined to find out why somebody killed him. She wants everything to be fair and just. Like you do, Sam. That's one reason she likes you. Now that Carmody's dead and you think somebody killed him, I'm afraid she might do something...ill-advised."

"She's so stubborn. Why can't she relax and let SAPD handle it? When I lost my family, there was nothing fair and just about that. If this is murder, and Aggie gets herself involved and we lose her..." He hung his head. "I just don't know..."

It touched me that Sam was worried, but I thought he and Meredith had talked enough. I made noise in the dressing room getting my clothes on and gave Sam plenty of time to disappear before I opened the door to the hall.

"How was the MRI?" Meredith said, her eyes wide in an expressionless face.

"It was loud. Let's go see what the doctors say happened to my head."

They reported a mild concussion with residual swelling. They didn't expect any permanent damage. I had to be careful and protect my head. Other than that, I could resume normal activity.

All right then. I could concentrate on more important matters.

Twenty-Four

With all the trauma going on, I hadn't worked out in ages and felt like a slug. But I had to go to class Thursday to see how everyone was reacting to Dr. Carmody's death.

Eric Lager was teaching the class. He smiled at me with his fishy leer and dove into an account of the history of genetics. He covered Tay-Sachs disease, a rare neurological disorder observed in the 1880s that attacked children between ages two and ten. Their nervous systems shut down and they died, rarely living past fifteen. They had inherited a defective copy of the HEXA gene from each parent.

Scientists had also discovered a mutated gene that caused Meryon's Disease, or Duchenne muscular dystrophy, a destructive neurological disease that affected only males and lead to death in their teens or twenties.

I'd read about these inherited diseases from links Dr. Carmody gave us. Dr. Eric Lager wasn't revealing any new information.

Brandy and Penelope gave me drop-dead looks. Brandy had more clothes on, and Penelope shot me penetrating stares. I'd just about worn out my welcome at UHT.

After class, Meredith and I met at Taco Bell for lunch.

We didn't have much to say to each other, so we chatted about the weather.

I knew she'd contacted Sam because she was worried about me, but I simply couldn't give her any more information. It would further complicate my life.

Once I got home, I was too agitated to study, so I decided to go to Fit and Firm on the Austin Highway and attempt to get back into shape. I donned new Adidas and my best-looking workout clothes, in case I saw a gorgeous male who could take my mind off Sam.

The treadmill I chose had a TV attached. I turned it on, flipped through channels and managed to walk at a moderate pace for forty-five minutes. I couldn't stop thinking about Carmody's demise. Had he inadvertently squirted fungus up his nose? Or had somebody actually killed him?

I'd have to eventually return to that lab and, unfortunately, I was less fit than usual. I had a knot on my head which I was supposed to protect, and Eric Lager gave me the creeps. After my treadmill session, I got off and strolled aimlessly around the gym, hoping I'd find a class to inspire me.

In one room, Zumba dancers gyrated to Latin music. I didn't think I should gyrate. Another group stepped frantically on and off risers. Too dangerous. I'd trip.

In a room toward the back of the gym, a man instructed a small group of women. I read the sign on the glass: "Self-Defense for Women. Instructor: Retired SAPD Sergeant Igor Koslov." Perfect. I needed to learn to protect myself if attacked. My head didn't need another concussion. Maybe this man could teach me how to defend myself and give me a dose of courage.

I walked straight to the reception desk and signed up for his Friday morning class.

Twenty-Five

When I walked through the door at eight forty-five a.m. Friday morning, sweaty, satisfied people were already pouring out of Fit and Firm. I showed my membership card and hustled straight back to Sergeant Igor Koslov's class, eager to master self-defense. He spoke to each of as we entered and handed us health and permission forms. I smiled.

"You're no longer with SAPD?"

"No. I retired five years ago. I do private security consulting now."

"So you don't get to hang out with the officers anymore?" I produced my friendliest conspiratorial smile.

Igor gave me a quizzical look. "Not really. If I have a question about a case, I drop by. Do you know some of the officers?"

"No. Just curious. I think it's great that an experienced man like you is teaching this class." I sat down to fill out the papers. Sam had applied to SAPD about the time Koslov had left. I was safe.

Eight women dribbled in, including Brandy Crystal, in short shorts and a sleeveless top over an actual bra. I wasn't surprised to see her here. Her hair lay on her head, unspiked, and she wasn't wearing makeup—a definite improvement. She saw me, grunted and dismissively waved a few fingers.

Once we'd given our names and addresses, swore we were not incapacitated, were capable of physical exertion and would not sue the club, Koslov cleared his throat and gathered us around him in a large circle.

"Let's talk about targets you aim for when someone attacks you. Combining the first letter of each target spells N-E-E-T-T, letters to help you remember where to attack." He gestured to class member Winifred to help him demonstrate. Winifred looked like she was tough enough to fight anybody.

"Nose: hit it straight up with your palm up." When Koslov's beefy palm stopped just short of breaking Winifred's nose, she started to blink and her eyes watered.

Koslov chose Sasha, a lanky brunette in stretch leggings, for the next demonstration, and put his hands about six inches from both sides of her head.

"Ears: Pop his ears from the sides with open palms. You can break his eardrums." Igor grinned. With her long arms, Sasha had enough leverage and power to deafen six-foot-tall Igor. At five foot four, I'd have to stand on tiptoes to reach his ears.

He beckoned a diminutive blonde, Annie, who was shorter than me.

"Eyes," he told Annie. "Stick your fingers right in them." She had to reach up, but with pointed nails and her arm straightened military style, her thrust could cause damage. Igor beckoned me over.

"I'm Aggie."

He sized me up. "Throat: Hold your hand like you're grasping a large cup. Stiffen your hand and whack my throat as hard as you can with the yolk of your hand."

I practiced a couple of times.

"Stiffen your arm," he said. "Hit harder."

After my third pretend whack, I was getting into it. A person could learn to enjoy this.

He chose Brandy for the next demo. He had her raise her arms and hold her fists outside his temples while he tried not to look at her chest.

"Temple: With the bottom of your fists, smash my temples hard." Brandy performed like a natural. "Remember, when an assailant approaches you, think N-E-E-T-T—nose, ears, eyes, throat, temple—and go for the closest targets. Scream while you're doing it. If you're close enough, stomp his foot. If he has piercings in his nose or ears, yank them out."

Could I do that? If the assailant started bleeding, I'd faint, and he'd kill me.

"If you can get in position, kick hard and push through his knee. That will stop anybody. As soon as he lets go of you, run."

I could do that.

Igor got the others involved and had us mimic attacks with different partners. Paired with Brandy, I enjoyed considering which move to try and actually wished I could deck her. Jealousy was a terrible thing.

"When you're walking to your car, day or night," he said, "hold your keys with one or two keys sticking through your fingers, sharp ends pointed out. If somebody accosts you, aim for their eyes and scratch them with the keys. Be aware of your surroundings. Carry a small flashlight in your purse. With your keys positioned in your hand, shine the light around before you get close to your car, Assailants look for somebody who's not paying attention."

I felt stupid for having been so vulnerable.

"Suppose an assailant grabs you from behind and traps your arms. Throw your head back as hard as you can to hit his face. If he doesn't let go, bite his arm. When your arms are free, go for a target. Stomp his foot. Knee him in the groin. Never quit fighting. As soon he steps back, take off screaming.

"If he grabs around you from the front, head-butt his nose or chin or push both arms up fast to break his hold. When he lets go, pop his eardrums with your palms and run screaming.

"Remember, if he chokes you from the front, don't grab his hands. He'll choke you harder until you pass out. If he chokes you from behind, claw at his hands or pop your arms up to break the hold and run screaming. If somebody slings his arm around your neck and traps you in a headlock, turn your head and bite his arm."

Practicing took a while. When we finished, we had moist faces and straggly hair. Igor could tell we were fading.

"So," he concluded, "you are equipped with a lot of weapons: your forehead, teeth, elbows, palms and fingers, yolk of your hand, outside edge of your fist, feet, legs and knees. Don't ever hit an assailant with your closed fist thrust forward. You'll break your hand. Use your hands the way I taught you."

We'd absorbed all Igor could teach us. I felt more confident but knew I'd have to practice the moves many times to be able to use them.

When I walked out of the gym, Brandy walked through the door at the same moment.

"So," I said, "did you enjoy meeting Detective Vanderhoven?"

She sliced her eyes at me, then looked straight ahead. "Not really."

"You couldn't help him learn who or what killed Dr. Carmody? The medical examiner says he didn't die of a stroke or heart attack."

She raised her eyebrows, then squinted her eyes into slits and clamped her jaw. "Well. That's comforting to know, now isn't it?" She stormed around me and charged full steam to her car.

It's funny how life offers up tiny nuggets. I'd learned a lot more than self-defense. I'd learned Brandy didn't like Sam, probably because she couldn't seduce him. She knew that Carmody didn't die from obvious causes. Even better, she knew that I knew. Of course, she could have known already. If she killed him.

Twenty-Six

I woke up Saturday morning with stiff legs from Thursday's treadmill workout and sore arms from mimicking poking people in the eyes, popping eardrums and breaking noses. Despite being grumpy and in pain, this was the ideal day to break into the lab. Even if students worked there Saturday, and I doubted there were many, the lab would shut down around dusk. I could sneak in after dark.

Carmody's killer was making my life miserable. Whatever was in that lab was what I'd worked for, written about and suffered for at the gym. If I didn't discover what Carmody discovered about aging, I'd be without hope and grow old fast. I might as well tell Sam the truth and forget about being loved. He thought I was grumpy and irrational anyway from the blow to my head. I should probably just keep my distance from him.

If I went back to the lab, he'd be furious, and if the killer was there, I might not make it out. Maybe it was better that my relationship with Sam had stalled.

Back in Chicago, I honestly thought I loved Lester. But when he found out I was pregnant and dropped me like a hot poker, I knew what a sap I'd been. I couldn't bring myself to abort the baby. It was innocent, and it was mine. But I couldn't keep it either. I couldn't earn enough to support us. We'd be on welfare.

Katy and Sam Vanderhoven didn't think they could have children and had decided to adopt. I knew they couldn't resist the offer of a child. They were desperate for a baby. Here was one they could have. Sam was never to know how the unexpected blessing came about. I made Katy promise never to tell him.

While I transferred to a branch bank to take a leave of absence, Katy's doctor delivered my baby, and Katy's lawyer legalized her adoption. By the time I returned to the main bank in Chicago, Sam and Katy Vanderhoven had adopted my baby girl and named her Lee.

I watched Katy and Sam delight in raising her. Until the horrible night when she and Katy were killed in that tragic auto accident.

Sam and I grieved separately. For the second time, I grieved over losing my child.

Sam and I didn't communicate after their funeral. Our shared memories were too painful. After a year, he called me to report he couldn't bear Chicago any longer and was moving to Texas for the warm weather.

When a large bank bought my smaller one, my bank stock made me unexpectedly prosperous. After six months of contemplating options, I moved to Texas. I'd always loved Sam. This was my last chance to see if he could love me.

I scrambled three eggs to ingest enough protein. At least my head didn't hurt and the lump was gone. The doctor had said to protect my head. Should I wear a hard hat—maybe a riding hat—in case I got whacked again? Riding helmets probably cost a fortune.

Gibson's Costume Shop probably had some, but they wouldn't be real. Meredith had jumped horses in competition; she probably owned an equestrian helmet. I dialed her number.

"Hey. What are you doing this morning?" I asked.

"Nothing much, just cleaning up. I have to shop for groceries. How's your head?"

"Much better. I'm just lollygagging around. Do you think I should wear a hard hat, like your riding hat, just in case?"

"My equestrian hat? In case of what? Why would you do that, unless you're going to do some kind of calisthenics? You're not going to do that, are you? Are you all right, Aggie?"

"I'm fine. I'm not doing anything physical. Really. I just thought...never mind. It was a dumb idea. I'll hang around the house and read."

"You're sure? If you've having symptoms, we should call the doctor."

"No, no. It was a silly thought. Really. I'm fine. My head doesn't even hurt. And the lump is almost gone."

"Well, if you're sure."

"I'm good. You know me and my harebrained ideas. Have a great day, okay?"

"All right, then. You too."

She sounded hesitant. I probably shouldn't have called her.

Twenty-Seven

I considered the details of breaking into the lab. I'd have to go at night, hope my dental implement could open the locked science building and lab, and that nobody was working there or lurking around. I'd look for evidence of Dr. Carmody's research and some clue to who killed him. But I'd have to search without knowing exactly what I hoped to find. I absolutely couldn't get caught.

What if the killer was there?

I had to make a choice. I could live miserably in hopes Sam suddenly decided he couldn't function without me. Or I could take matters into my own hands and help solve this crime. I was in a unique position to find clues, I wanted justice for Dr. Carmody, and I'd never been one to wait around. I'd go for it.

Standing before the full-length mirror in my bedroom, I worked on looking determined and tough. Repeating N-E-E-T-T, I thrust fingers at my eyes in the mirror, popped my image's eardrums, shoved the heel of my hand at her nose, cupped my hand and aimed for her throat. Balling my fists, I whacked her temples from the side. Hard.

I prayed the attacker didn't have any piercings I'd have to yank out.

Staring at myself in the mirror, I didn't think I looked very formidable.

Was it worth risking my life to help solve Carmody's murder? Probably not. But if I combined that with saving my own future...

* * *

I fiddled around all day resting, worrying, planning, reading and eating peanut butter. What should I wear? What should I take besides the dental pick?

After trying on every black outfit I owned, I settled on a cotton t-shirt with long sleeves, the lightest-weight black pants I possessed (so I wouldn't suffocate from the heat) and a black Jimmy cap to stuff my hair under. I arranged the hat with the sore spot located at the back vent, which would be perfect if I didn't get whacked on the head again. When I touched the spot, it felt nearly normal.

I was perfectly clad and unrecognizable, a poster for breaking and entering. I had the bright idea to rub dark makeup on my face, neck and wrists to further disguise myself. My hands needed to be free; they were weapons. I found a pair of thin black gloves.

Next, I concentrated on what to carry in my pants pockets: dental pick and a nail file (in case the implement didn't work.) If I determined I shouldn't turn on the lab lights, I'd need a small flashlight.

Changing into shorts and a tank top, I raced to Sunset Ridge Home and Hardware to purchase a high-intensity, small beam flashlight and found another necessary item: a package of thin, surgical-weight cleaning gloves. I could not afford to leave fingerprints.

I drove home and paced in front of the TV. Shopping had used up a little time. I was too antsy to read. If I ate any more, I'd be sick. Darkness wouldn't descend until almost nine p.m.

Obsessed with my breaking-and-entering plans, I hadn't even thought about the mail. There was a pile growing by the front door. I swooped it up, thumbed through and found a letter to Dear Aggie with a postmark several days old. The reader might think Aggie absconded with the mail man. What if she knew she'd written to somebody about to commit a break-in? I opened it.

Dear Aggie,

I used to be optimistic—fearless—always looking toward the future. I realized I'll be fifty in February and should probably start acting like it. It's kind of unseemly for a matron to eagerly gallivant through life, don't you think? Being proper and staid isn't much fun though. In fact, it's getting depressing.

Aging and Ambivalent in Akron,
Ariel

Dear Ariel,

Don't be ambivalent. Enjoy life. You might have half a lifetime yet to go. Why shouldn't you enjoy it? Figure out what you've always wanted to do, then set yourself on a path to do it. We humans are weird. We're always figuring out how we should be, then we plod along trying to act like that. That's a recipe guaranteed to bore others. Not to mention yourself. You're as old as you believe you are. You're as young as your curiosity, your dreams, and your determination.

Ever Expectant,
Aggie

Twenty-Eight

Activated by Ariel in Akron, I started getting dressed at eight p.m. I put on the black garb first, then arranged my hair under the hat. I spread the utensils among my pockets so they weren't lumpy.

I traipsed to my bedroom bookshelf and picked up *An In-Depth History of the World*. The tome looked like it had at least a thousand pages, so nobody ever picked it up. Actually, it was a hollow hiding place for the bracelet they'd put on my baby's arm in the hospital. It had become my good luck charm; I took it with me to face momentous events. I had to cut and re-tape the bracelet to fit it around my wrist.

I put on black socks and dark tennis shoes, and hoped my feet would stop itching. I'd have to keep my car keys in a pocket during the break-in. I wrapped them in tissue so they wouldn't jingle.

In the garage, I saw heavy-duty twine I'd bought for another project and decided to take it in case I had to tie somebody up. After locking my driver's license, money and credit card in the glove compartment, I started Albatross and drove to the university.

By a little past eight thirty on Saturday night, most students would have left. The school should be deserted and quiet.

I eased onto the campus through a side entrance, seeing few cars and people. It was nearly dark. One parking lot contained a few cars. Lovers smooched inside one of them. The girl reminded me of Brandy. Was she with the same scientist or a different one? Why didn't they just go up to her plush apartment? Maybe it wasn't her. I had Brandy on the brain.

Lights from the library glowed in the distance, and a few trees were lighted. The clock tower cast an eerie glow over the sleeping campus.

I crept toward the science building. Slowing near the rear entrance, I prayed my dental pick would unlock the door. I parked half a block from the building, cut the motor and pulled on the black gloves.

When I opened the car door, I started to hyperventilate. I closed the door and sat still to gain control. Taking deep breaths, I told myself again why I was there and what would occur if I didn't follow through with my mission. After mentally practicing N-E-E-T-T, I patted my pockets to take inventory. This time I scanned the area before emerging from the car. No one was around.

Holding my keys with sharp ends pointed out, I tiptoed through shadows toward the back of the building. A light shone above the door, but it was dark to either side. Positioning my body so that only my black glove and arm were under the light, I pushed the dental pick into the lock and twisted. I heard a click, pulled the heavy door open and slipped inside.

Twenty-Nine

I had to orient myself to the dark interior of the building and find the lab. I was on the main floor with the laboratory. Unless a hallway branched off, if I continued straight down the hall, the doors to both the small storage room and lab should be on my left. I inched along with one finger touching the wall at intervals to make sure I stayed on track.

I'd taken only about ten steps when I heard a noise and froze. Flattening myself against the wall, I waited, my breath coming in short jerks. Someone was opening the door at the front of the building, the main entrance. I heard them click the lock and saw them shine a light inside and enter. The intruder eased the heavy door closed and came toward me down the hall. A flashlight beam danced eight feet in front of the hulk. Another fifty feet and he couldn't help but see me.

Slithering to the right toward the back door where I'd entered, I moved silently as fast as I could, with my right hand feeling for the wall. If I could get close enough to the door before he saw me, I could slip through and hide outside in the dark before he figured out what he'd heard.

I'd almost reached the back door when the flashlight beam vanished. I stopped and held my breath. The light reappeared down the hall in front of me, shining on a doorway at the right side of the hall. The beam moved down to the door's keypad, and a gloved hand unlocked the door. The figure slipped inside and turned on lights inside the room.

I took a huge breath and expelled a sigh. Some professor must have needed to work late. Students and professors used to frequently work after hours, but the university had suffered financial difficulties and was saving energy to cut costs. Most campus buildings were now dark at night except for the library, recreational facility and parking garage. Buildings had lights shining on entry doors or placed sporadically around the exterior, but interior lights were off, and professors and students were discouraged from working at night.

Whoever entered the room had a key to the building and classroom and was familiar with the layout. So why enter in the dark? Perhaps if they worked late, against university policy, they got a black mark. No tenure? Thus, the dark gloves.

I had a choice to make: go out the back door and forget the whole project, or sneak past the working professor where light streamed into the hall and hope I could make it into the lab undetected.

Option number two won. I started sneaking left again, glued to the wall. When I got near the lighted classroom, I was tempted to peek in and see who was there. It might be somebody I knew. But if they saw me, I could be arrested for breaking and entering. I put my curiosity on hold.

The classroom light carried only halfway across the hall, so before I reached the lighted area, I crouched down as low as I could on the left-hand wall and wiggled past the light looming from the right. When I glanced back, I couldn't see anybody inside the classroom.

I estimated that in about eight more feet, I'd reach the door that entered the long narrow room with the UV light apparatus. I got to the door and hesitated. I couldn't linger—the professor might decide he was through working and step into the hall. But I had to be sure of my surroundings.

When I'd entered the building to meet Eric Lager, the lab door was the first door to the right from the front entrance. From where I stood, I could see a door ten feet ahead that I was pretty sure was the door to the main lab. For a few seconds, a touch of moonlight shone through glass in the building's front door and confirmed it. This door next to me was the linear storage room with the ultraviolet light over the tray, the room I wanted. If somebody entered the main door to the lab, I could escape through this back door. I inserted my dental pick, heard a click and slipped inside, leaving the door slightly ajar.

Thirty

I clicked on my flashlight, shone a small beam just ahead of my feet and tiptoed across the storage room. I wanted to check everything in the room where I was, but first I had to make sure there was nobody in the lab. I doused my light, crept to the open door between the rooms and peered in. There was no sound. No light. It was safe to investigate.

I peeled off the black gloves, slipped them into my pocket, pulled on the thin latex pair and retraced my steps to where I'd entered. From there, I shone my light on each cabinet. I didn't see anything new. One wall cabinet had drawers beneath, so I opened each one soundlessly. Nothing but supplies. It was time for the main event.

Walking silently into the large room, I smelled the familiar medicinal odor. The lab must have been sterilized, but I detected a slightly rank smell with an overlay of sweetness the cleaning liquid hadn't erased.

In the dark, I sensed the mass of the box-like 37°C incubator hugging the wall. I bent to crack open the incubator door and shone my light inside. The sight of living cells quivering in plates, floating in unknown liquid, mutating at human body temperature, made me queasy. Were they worm cells? Human cells? Squirming in what? I knew I was viewing a common research practice, but the way Eric Lager described cell reproduction with his fish grin made the process seem tawdry and evil, as though unnatural metamorphoses were developing before my eyes.

I decided to systematically check every cabinet and drawer moving right from the incubator. I got close to each cabinet to shine the light inside. I didn't want my flashlight to illuminate the room. The drawers contained office supplies, rubber tubing, order sheets—nothing revealing: no notes and no list of scientists. When I looked through drawers under the shade-drawn windows, I was particularly careful with my light. The campus police or a caretaker might see light in the science lab and decide to investigate.

After examining drawers across the back side of the lab, I decided to backtrack and search through drawers and cabinets that ran from the incubator toward the front wall that separated the lab from the hallway. The storage areas yielded nothing, but a cut in the countertop made space for a desk and computer.

I set my flashlight down to one side and aimed it at the screen. Pulling the chair out slowly, I eased into it and studied the equipment. I located the sound button and turned it off. I didn't want the machine blaring my presence into the hallway. I hit the "On" button and watched the computer power up with Office 97 and Internet Explorer 3.0. First, I went to IE3 to search through Bookmarks.

I found links to articles about daf-2 and daf-16 genes, APOE genes related to Alzheimer's disease, telomeres, telomerase, *C. elegans* roundworms and earmarks for aging—all subjects I knew Carmody had researched. How could I determine which lead he'd decided to pursue? The discovery that probably got him killed?

My best guess was that he'd been experimenting with ways to alter specific genes and was recording the results. But he probably had the information encoded. I pulled up the list of programs.

The university used the Bio101 program, a new integrative teaching tool where students could see molecules and cells interacting with stimuli. I called up the program, but to enter it required a password. I tried "K.Carmody@UHT.edu" and every other version of his name I could think of. Nothing worked. He must have filed the revealing information somewhere, but I didn't know what else to try. Feeling defeated and increasingly aware of the sickly sweet odor and strong disinfectant, I closed down the computer.

I decided to make a final pass around the other side of the room toward the main lab door that led to the hall. I retraced my steps around the periphery, past the shaded windows, and down the first set of cabinets and drawers, inching toward the front door. I'd searched through three drawers and cabinets and stepped toward the next section when my foot hit a barrier on the floor. I shone my light on the object and screamed.

Thirty-One

Eric Lager lay on the laboratory floor with his feet toward me and his head near the door. The lower part of his body appeared relaxed, as if his muscles had withered. The upper part of his thin torso appeared stiff. His face, usually gray and colorless, had a pink tinge. He was obviously dead. One arm stretched toward the door. Just outside the reach of his hand lay a bottle of nasal spray.

Unable to take my eyes off Eric Lager, with the sickly sweet odor of death and disinfectant permeating my senses, I felt sick. Paralyzed with shock, I covered my mouth and tried to remember the location of the nearest sink. I was feeling my way back across countertops when the hall door blasted open.

"Police! Stop! Let me see your hands!"

I tried to raise my hands, but I had to grab the nearest sink to upchuck into it. I was leaning on the counter, splashing water on my face as two uniformed police officers marched toward me shining flashlights. One had his gun drawn. Neither one of them was Sam.

Dizzy and disoriented, I felt blackness overtake me.

When I regained consciousness, I was sitting against a cabinet with an officer crouched beside me.

"I'm Officer Mangum, SAPD." He pointed up to another man in a different uniform. "Grant is from campus security. And you are?"

"Aggie...Agatha Mundeen. I'm a student here."

"What were you doing in this lab?" Mangum asked.

"Looking for clues to who killed Dr. Carmody and to what he was working on."

"Carmody was the professor who died on campus last week?"

"Yes, sir. Somebody at SAPD found out he'd been murdered."

"And you broke into this lab because...?"

"Well, it was locked. And I didn't want anybody to know."

"Know what? That you killed a man?"

"No! I would never kill anybody. After I learned Dr. Carmody was murdered, I thought it must have something to do with whatever he was working on here."

"I imagine the police could figure that out. But you decided to dress in black, smear your face dark, break into a locked campus facility and look for clues. You're a science student?"

"Well, no."

"So you probably wouldn't recognize clues in here anyway. Is that what you're telling us?"

I nodded, realizing how dumb I sounded.

"Do you know who that man is?" He pointed to Lager.

"Professor Eric Lager."

"Another professor who worked at UHT?"

"I'm afraid so." I feared I might be sick again. "Could you take me outside and let me get some air?"

"In a minute. You know this professor?" He gestured toward Eric Lager.

I couldn't look at his body. "Yes. He was the lab director. He took over Dr. Carmody's class." I didn't tell him that Eric had invited me to tour the lab. It might sound like Eric and I had a closer relationship.

"You want me to believe that you broke in here, knowing Lager might be here, and you didn't have anything to do with his murder?"

"Yes, sir. I mean, no, sir. I didn't have any idea he'd be here."

"But you broke in, and there he was?"

"I was walking around in the dark, and I bumped into him...his leg, I guess."

He studied my face before speaking. "Have you ever been arrested before?"

"No, sir."

More SAPD officers streamed in. Not one of them was Sam.

"All right." Mangum stood me up and beckoned to a female patrolman. "Officer Ames, search this woman."

Ames looked young enough to be my daughter. She came over, cleared her throat and maintained a poker face while she began her body search. In front of everybody.

She found my black gloves, peeled the thin ones off my hands and put each pair in a separate bag. She found my dental implement, nail file and flashlight, and squinted at me suspiciously while she bagged them. After handing the stash to another officer, she repeated her pat-down.

More policemen arrived, dusted for fingerprints, took photos and looked for blood and other evidence around Lager's body. One picked up the nasal spray bottle and bagged it.

UHT's campus security man, Grant, cupped a hand in front of his mouth and spoke quietly to Officer Mangum. "Hey, can y'all try to keep this to a minimum? This looks bad for the university since we had another professor die here last week. If we have a bunch of raging lights and sirens, the press will come swarming around here. We don't want students to feel like they're in danger. How long do you think it'll be before EMS comes for the body and you fellows finish up? Students will want to work in the lab tomorrow morning. Some of them expect us to open up by seven a.m."

"I'll ask EMS to douse the lights and siren," Mangum said. "We can probably finish up here pretty soon. We'll leave an officer outside the lab tonight and one outside the building to control who goes in and out. In the morning, they can tell students there was a suspected break-in, but that everything's okay."

He gestured to the female officer.

"Ames, you and Grant take this suspect out behind the building for some air and stay with her. Homicide's on the way. Keep her on the premises. I'll talk to her later."

Homicide? I could see where I might be in trouble for breaking and entering, but surely they didn't think I'd killed Eric Lager. If Homicide was on the way, maybe it would be Sam.

Ames and Grant each grabbed one of my arms, tighter than I thought was necessary. Mangum drew my hands together and handcuffed me. Me! Aggie Mundeen. I was just looking for clues to a murder.

While I tried not to cry, Ames and Grant walked me through the back door and outside to the lawn.

"Let's wait over there in the dark," Grant said. "No need to attract attention."

Thirty-Two

We were hidden in darkness with only the light from the back door of the science building reflecting off nearby grass. Ames and Grant sat me down and perched a few feet away on either side. I saw a van roll onto the campus road.

"There's EMS," Ames said. The vehicle slinked around the side of the building, turned off its lights and parked. Three figures emerged from the van with a stretcher and quietly approached the front of the building. Two cars rolled up and parked behind the van: Meredith's car and a familiar car I thought might be Sam's unmarked sedan. As they approached, I said a silent prayer of thanks. They could get me out of this mess.

Sam strolled up in plainclothes and a cap with the bill pulled down. Meredith was behind him.

"Hello, officers," he said and pulled out his badge. "Detective Sam Vanderhoven, Homicide, SAPD. And this is Meredith Laughlin." He pointed to me. "This woman is a friend of ours. Okay if we speak with her?"

"She was studying and passed out in the science lab," Grant said. "No big deal. UHT has everything under control. You want to talk to her? Sure."

Officer Ames looked at Sam and Meredith. "Your names and addresses, please." She took out her pad.

Meredith gave her address and phone number.

"You've known her long?" Ames said.

"We've had some classes together."

She turned to Sam. "And you, Detective?"

"We're more like acquaintances," Sam said.

"Why did you show up here in the middle of the night?"

"I couldn't sleep," Meredith said. "I knew Aggie was upset about Dr. Carmody, the man who died here last week. I called her, and she didn't answer. I decided to call Detective Vanderhoven and drive over here. We saw her sitting with you guys here on the lawn."

Officer Ames stuffed her pad back in her pocket. "Detective, just let me know what she says."

"Sure thing."

Sam and Meredith came over and crouched on either side of me. Sam's back was to Ames. Grant surveyed the campus as if he was worried about who might show up and create bad PR for the school.

"Aggie," Meredith said. "Are you okay? You're handcuffed."

I nodded.

Sam put a finger to his lips, indicating I should talk quietly and be careful what I said.

"She said you fainted," Sam said in a low voice, almost whispering. "Tell me what happened."

"I snuck into the lab to find out who killed Dr. Carmody...or figure out what he was working on. Eric Lager was lying on the floor. Dead. They must think I killed him. I guess that's why I have on these ridiculous handcuffs."

"Did you see anybody around?"

My head was pounding so hard, it was difficult to think. "Somebody was in the room across the hall—some professor, I guess."

"Did you see who it was?"

"No. I was too busy trying to..."

"Sneak into the lab?"

"Yes."

"Did you find anything?"

"No." I sighed and closed my eyes. The universe spun.

"When did you first see Eric Lager?"

Officer Ames flipped her head toward us. I lowered my voice. "I was checking cabinets in the dark, shining my light inside them. Campus security must have noticed the light and called SAPD. My foot hit something...Eric's leg. I shined my flashlight on him and screamed. Then cops burst through the door."

"Was he dead when you first saw him?"

"Yes. He looked horrible." I opened my eyes. "How did you two know to come here?

We heard the sound of another vehicle, and Ames looked toward the road.

"Somebody from the medical examiner's office," she said.

Sam whispered, "When you wanted to borrow a riding helmet from Meredith, she guessed you were up to something and called me. I surmised you came to the campus. But I didn't think you'd break into the lab dressed like a burglar and stumble on a corpse."

"I never dreamed..." I blinked, trying to block the image of Eric Lager lying on the floor: gray, pink, half limp, half stiff and very dead.

I was telling Sam about the nasal spray bottle I'd seen within reach of Eric's hand when I realized his voice had sounded different. I looked at him.

"What happens now?"

"When somebody breaks into a building and is found with a dead body, the police take them to jail." He talked louder, probably for Officer Ames' benefit.

"To jail?" I whispered. "You can't mean that. You know I didn't kill Eric Lager." He put his hand to his lips to quiet me. "I couldn't kill anybody. You can just tell them." He kept the finger to his lips.

Meredith and I looked at him pleadingly.

"It's not that simple." He talked in a fast whisper. "Law officers have to go by evidence. You argued with Carmody before he was murdered. Some people thought you contributed to his death."

I scowled at him.

"Eric Lager is another of your professors. You broke into the university lab, in the dark, dressed in black to avoid detection, and were found at the feet of a dead man who was probably murdered. I don't see how you can avoid being charged with trespass, burglary...possibly murder."

Meredith's hand covered her mouth. "I should have stopped her, Sam. I should have called you sooner."

Ames glanced over.

"What Aggie did isn't your fault, Meredith," Sam whispered, shaking his head. "There seems to be no stopping her."

I rubbed my wrists together and realized my baby's bracelet was missing. Her hospital bracelet, my only link to her, the bracelet I'd cherished as my talisman for years, was gone. And I couldn't search for it. It appeared I'd lost my baby a third time. My luck had run out. Tears spilled down my cheeks.

"You'll go with me, won't you, Sam? To jail? To vouch for me?"

"That's not possible, Aggie." I could barely hear him. "Officers are forbidden from involvement in a case not associated with their assigned duties. I haven't been assigned to this case. I didn't even know Eric Lager was dead. If I involve myself with a friend charged with a crime, it's a major rule violation. I'd be suspended and probably kicked out of the department. While the night detective works the scene, the patrolman dispatched here first will transport you to Central Police Station, then to be magistrated."

"You knew I'd probably be here? And you let me get arrested? Without my even going home first?" I knew I sounded illogical and pathetic. I was getting desperate. How could my friend...maybe even my future husband...desert me? My life was ruined. I wished I'd died with Eric Lager.

When Sam leaned closer, his hair flopped on his forehead. "Believe me, Aggie, I'd give anything if you hadn't done this. But you did. I have to follow the law."

I wished I could see his doggy eyes better behind the tortoise-shell glasses so I'd know if they held any sympathy at all.

"I hoped I was wrong about your being here," he whispered. "If I stay at the scene too long where a crime occurred, the department might think I'm involved. Then I can't help either one of us."

"Can I go with her," Meredith asked, "and vouch for her, or try to post bond or something?"

Sam shook his head. "You can't go with her. Neither can I."

He walked over to Officer Ames. "Looks like she got too curious and decided to find out why that other professor died. Bad timing. I know you have a job to do."

She nodded and made a note on her pad.

Thirty-Three

We heard the EMS van's engine start and saw two men carrying a stretcher toward the vehicle. Grant walked over to Officer Ames. "Poor devil. At least they're being quiet about it. Enrollment is already down. We don't need a media circus around here."

Everyone had agendas. Even when a man—two men—had been murdered. Light from the back door of the building flooded across the lawn. Officer Mangum approached.

"We're about done here, Officer Ames." He saw Meredith. "Who are you?"

"Aggie's friend, Meredith Laughlin."

I heard a car start near the EMS van and did not look in that direction.

"I interviewed her," Ames said, looking pleased, "and got her contact info. They're classmates. Detective Vanderhoven, SAPD Homicide, talked with her too." She looked around. Sam was gone. Ames shrugged. "He was another friend of this woman—not on the case."

"And why were they here?"

"They were apparently worried about her, couldn't get her on the phone, came to look around campus and spotted her on the lawn."

"Okay, Officer Ames. Give me your report. I've got the other information. Charge is burglary. Pending toxicology, homicide may be added later. I'll take Ms. Mundeen down to Central Station. You can go back on patrol."

He gave UHT's security guard a card. "Thanks for your help, Officer Grant. Call us if you think of anything. We'll be in touch."

Mangum took my arms, with me still handcuffed, in front of Meredith and Ames and Grant, and steered me toward his patrol car. I was mortified. At least it was nighttime and the whole student body wasn't ogling the spectacle of a mature student being hauled off.

I looked up at Officer Mangum's expressionless face. With his less-than-generous spirit, I'd think of him as Officer Magnanimous. I knew I shouldn't have broken into Dr. Carmody's apartment and into the lab, but my intentions were good. I only took his papers to try to find his killer. Now I was arrested for burglary and suspected of homicide? I never thought this could happen.

"What happens at Central? What does it mean 'to be magistrated?'"

Magnanimous ignored my questions and opened the back door of his car. I felt his hand on my head—fortunately, not on the sore spot. I remembered seeing criminals on TV being eased into squad cars so they didn't hit their heads. Criminals. Who stole for their own benefit or who hurt people.

I thought I was going to pass out. I couldn't possibly go to jail. With criminals.

There was a partition between me and Magnanimous, but I could see through it out the front of the vehicle. His radio squawked occasionally.

He drove off the campus and turned south on Broadway. I gawked through the front and side windows, wondering how long it would be before I drove down this street again. I stared at every landmark so I wouldn't forget it.

We cruised by ButterKrust Bakery. I'd heard the company had been sold and would stop baking bread. For now, it was lighted from within with bakers and machinery working through the night. Inhaling the pungent aroma of baking bread almost made me cry.

We headed toward downtown San Antonio. Instead of getting on Highway 281 South, he stayed on Broadway until it turned into

Losoya. Maybe he wanted to show a police presence downtown, or maybe he enjoyed driving through the heart of the city seeing the lights and living vicariously with late-night tourists who weren't going to jail. He continued to Commerce Street and turned right. We drove past entrances to the San Antonio River Walk and saw lights twinkling from restaurants at river level. Would I ever celebrate there again?

The imposing façade of San Fernando Cathedral loomed on a street to our left. Not far after that, just before Commerce Street rose in an arc in front of us, he got into the left lane and swung onto Frio Street.

Frio was lined with buildings. I was surprised to see Double Tree Inn on the left next to a building which was part of the University of Texas at San Antonio's downtown campus. UTSA had a second building on the other side of the street. This might be as close as I'd ever get to a university again. I couldn't believe that instead of studying for Tuesday's class, I was in a patrol car.

Past UTSA, down a side street to the right, I saw two small decrepit buildings: River City Bonds and Country Bail Bonds. Surely, if they actually intended to put me in jail, I could post bond. I'd invested the money I earned at the bank, so my bank account held only what I needed for a few months' living expenses.

A huge building loomed ahead, the sign reading: "Frank D. Wing Municipal Court Building." Underneath, it read "Magistrate." Was that where I was going? Magnanimous turned left before he reached the court building and headed for the city's Central Service Area Police Department.

Thirty-Four

Office Mangum removed me from the backseat of his patrol car and walked me, handcuffed, into Central Police Station. The female officer just inside the door searched me again, while the officer at the desk watched, his dark eyes unreadable. How could I possibly have snatched anything with handcuffs on?

Mangum marched me to the desk, and I squinted at the desk officer's name tag: Detective Anthony Cruz. He raised his eyebrows.

"What do we have here?"

"A UHT security guard saw light in the science building and called SAPD," Mangum said. "Dispatch sent me to the university. When I arrived, I found the suspect near a victim in the lab. EMS arrived and pronounced him dead at nine forty-five p.m. The medical examiner arrived and processed the body for evidence. Then the contract ambulance took the body to the ME's office—autopsy will be held as soon as possible." He gestured toward me. "I have her listed on my report as actor in the burglary. Homicide said they'll take care of the rest after the ME determines cause and manner of death."

It was bad enough being pushed from place to place like a sack of meal. They talked about me like I wasn't standing right there. Actor in the burglary? I hadn't stolen anything from the lab. Homicide? Me? That was preposterous.

Cruz, evaluating me with unfriendly eyes, reached for the papers and called out, "Number one. Homicide."

They'd already decided I killed somebody?

Officer Mangum nudged me toward a row of metal chairs attached to each other that flanked the walls. Before I could sit, another officer appeared by the desk in plainclothes. His name tag read Detective Raymond Botowski. He reminded me of Igor, but he was smaller with sandy hair.

He took the papers from Officer Cruz. "I'll take her back. Mangum, I'll beep you when she's ready for transport."

"Number is 4-0-1-1. I'll be at Double Tree. Eating."

As Mangum fled to food and freedom, my stomach rumbled. I felt empty, but I didn't think food could maneuver around the lump in my throat. Botowski pointed me down a hall and walked behind me. "Third door on the right."

When he pushed open the door, I peered in. Metal desk. Neat except for stacks of folders in a tray. Comfortable looking, cushioned chair behind the desk. Hard metal chair in front of the desk. He pointed me toward it.

I went over, sat and waited while he flipped through pages.

"Agatha Emory Mundeen?"

I nodded.

"Says here you broke into the laboratory at UHT. Dressed in black with...let's see...rope, flashlight, nail file, dental implement used to pick locks and two pairs of gloves, wearing one pair."

I nodded.

"Have you ever been arrested?"

"No, sir."

"We'll run a criminal history. If you've ever been arrested, it will show up."

"You won't find anything."

He leaned back in his chair and studied me. "You don't look much like a burglar."

"I'm not."

"We'll see."

I needed to go to the bathroom, wash my hands and clean the dark makeup off my face. If they let me go, I'd probably be frisked again when I returned, so I crossed my legs.

Botowski combed through police reports, periodically glancing up at me. I was suddenly very tired. My throat lump slid down to join the jumping beans in my stomach.

He rearranged himself in his chair and motioned to an officer outside the door who heaved his bulk inside the doorframe.

"If I remove your handcuffs, you will remain seated in that chair," Botowski stated.

I nodded. He walked toward me and, with the supersized officer lurking, removed my handcuffs. I rubbed my wrists and stretched my shoulders forward.

"All right. Let's see how this goes." He clicked on a recorder, put his elbows on the desk, clasped one fist over the other and asked me to repeat my name and address. "You have the right to remain silent. Anything you say can be used against you in a court of law. You have the right to speak to an attorney and to have an attorney present during any questioning. If you cannot afford an attorney, one will be provided for you by the court."

"My friend is trying to find an attorney for me."

He leaned back in his chair. "You're a student at the university taking a science class?"

"Yes. Science of Aging." I rubbed my wrists and arms.

"Aren't you kind of old to be a student?"

I glared at him. "I write a column about staying young and want to learn about the genetic effects of aging."

"Hmm. But your story is that you picked the lock to the science building and lab dressed like a burglar to look for clues to another professor's murder that occurred a week ago?"

"Yes, sir."

"What did you expect to find?"

"I don't know. I thought somebody had killed Dr. Carmody—the first professor—because he was working in the lab to discover a genetic breakthrough to delay aging."

"And you were going to find this breakthrough?"

"I thought I might find something to suggest the direction of his research."

"Are you a scientist?"

"No, but..."

"How long have you been in this class?"

"A week."

"Uh-huh. And you were going to solve the other murder by burglarizing this lab?"

Heat rose up my neck. "I'm not a burglar. I didn't take anything."

"Burglary," he said, "is entering a building with intent to commit theft. Or committing theft or other felony without the consent of the owner."

I didn't have anybody's consent.

But I never planned to steal anything...maybe just borrow something that looked like a clue and take it to Sam. Like Carmody's papers.

I reminded myself not to bring up Sam's name.

"And when you broke into the lab, you didn't have any idea this other professor would be there?"

"That's right. Otherwise I'd never have gone in there."

"But you did know him, this Professor Eric Lager?"

"Yes. He was director of the lab and sometimes helped Dr. Carmody teach our class."

"Did you ever meet him outside of class?"

Was he insinuating there was a reason for me to kill Eric? I might as well tell him about the lab tour.

"I saw him at Dr. Carmody's funeral, and he invited me to tour the lab."

"Ah. So you did know him. How well did you know him?"

What he implied was disgusting. "I knew him only as student and professor."

"Why did you agree to tour the lab with him?"

"He probably knew what Dr. Carmody was working on. I thought I might get hints about what that was."

"So you learned a valuable secret and decided to kill the only other man who knew about it."

"No! I didn't learn any secret. When I went back tonight, I didn't know Eric Lager was even in there. And I didn't kill him. I stumbled into him, and he was dead." My heart beat like a hammer

He studied me. "I understand the first professor died from some kind of fungus in his nasal spray."

I nodded.

"Answer out loud for the tape recorder, please."

"Yes, sir."

"Officers found a bottle of nasal spray at the scene where you were found with the victim. Did you put it there?"

"No, I saw it near him when he was lying on the floor."

"Do you know what was in the bottle?"

"No." I hung my head. "I didn't kill Eric Lager. I'd never kill anybody."

"We'll find out what killed him from the autopsy and toxicology report. We'll request a quick turnaround on that. Then we'll know whether to charge you as a murder suspect."

"I told you. I could never commit murder."

He flipped through his notes and turned off the recorder. "All right." He punched numbers into his phone. "Mangum, she's ready to be magistrated."

"What happens there?" Would this nightmare ever be over?

"They'll put you in a nice comfortable cell while they compile the officers' reports. An assistant district attorney working night shift will review police reports to see if the facts support the charges against you. Then the clerks will gather everything for the magistrate, the Bexar County Judge who reads you your rights, lists charges against you and sets bond."

My eyes filled. "That could take a long time."

He crossed his arms. "Don't do something to get yourself arrested. Especially on Saturday night." He came over, told me to stand and handcuffed me.

"Can I call somebody?"

"You can make a call at the magistrate's."

I would call Meredith. I prayed she could help me.

Thirty-Five

Officer Botowski walked me down the hall and handed me back to Officer Mangum, who stood waiting beside the desk. It was almost two a.m.

I made it to the parking lot before I started crying.

"I told him I didn't kill anybody. Isn't anybody going to listen to me? They're going to put me in a cell at the magistrate's building. And the magistrate has nothing but police reports about me. Will I even get to talk to him?"

Mangum didn't say a word. He put his hand on my head and pushed me down into the backseat of his patrol car. I sniffed hot, angry tears. Any officer assigned to drive a vehicle for SAPD must be bordering on mute. He drove across the street to the Frank D. Wing Municipal Court Building. The building was lighted against a pitch black sky. He parked and escorted me through a side door into a large room where people handled papers behind a large, square enclosure. Without a word to me, he handed me over to another officer. "She was interviewed at Central."

The magistrate officer took me through another room and put me into a large cell behind it. About fifteen people sat slouched against the wall in the eight-by-twelve-foot enclosure. Some of them were sleeping. If their eyes were open, they were bloodshot or looked sad or vacant. I found a spot on the floor between two people who didn't smell too bad, put my head in my hands and sent up a silent prayer that if He'd help me get out of this mess, I promised never to break and enter again. And I waited.

"Mundeen," a man barked. "You want to make a call?"

I stood so fast I got dizzy and had to lean against the wall. I hadn't eaten for hours.

"Yes. Yes." I stumbled toward the officer before he changed his mind.

He put up a finger. "You get one call." He led me to a room with a chair, desk and phone. "Sit here." He crossed his arms and watched.

I dialed Meredith's number, knowing I'd wake her up.

"Meredith, I'm about to go to jail! I'm in the magistrate's building, but they let me out of the cell to call you. The judge is going to read charges against me—the police said 'burglary.' I didn't take anything, but they're going to take me to jail anyway. One said I might be a murder suspect. I'm probably waking you up. Does Sam know? You have to get me out of here."

"Aggie, I know, I know. I couldn't sleep. And Sam knows. He knows about the police reports and the charges and where you are. Everybody is taken to the magistrate from the police station. Sam told me to start finding you a lawyer as soon as the sun comes up. Once the magistrate sets your bond, Sam says the lawyer or I can bail you out. You won't have to stay in jail long."

"I don't want to stay in jail at all. How can you find a lawyer on Sunday? How much will bond be? I have some money, but it's tied up. You shouldn't have to pay to bail me out."

"I don't know how much it is. If it's a lot, I'll try to get it as soon as I can. When I find the lawyer, he'll know the charges and the amount of bond set by the judge. He'll advise us."

I started crying again. I didn't want to be advised. I wanted out of this miserable place. I wanted food and a bath at home with clean sheets and my friends to commiserate with me. I hoped Sam was still my friend.

I sniffed. "What did Sam say?"

"He said you should try to be brave. That he's getting the facts and figuring out the best way to help you. As your friend, he won't be officially assigned to the case, and he can't come see you in jail.

But he said SAPD would find out who killed Eric Lager and Dr. Carmody."

My feelings were mixed. At least Sam knew I didn't kill Lager. I'd move heaven and earth to help him. Shouldn't he do it for me? If he got too involved, he might lose his job. I understood that. I just didn't want it to be true because I needed him.

"Sam didn't comment on what I did?"

"No."

"Time's up, miss." The officer reached for my arm.

Meredith overheard. "I'll find a lawyer, Aggie…"

When I asked to use the bathroom, a female officer had to take me there. I scrubbed my face and hands with soap as best I could. If I didn't look so grubby, maybe the magistrate would take pity on me.

Thirty-Six

The officer took me back to the cell. I crumpled to my spot on the floor and waited, feeling somewhat better. My friends hadn't abandoned me; they knew where I was and they were trying to help.

Across the cell, four people sat together on the floor. They talked among themselves and seemed pretty casual about being there. Two men and a woman with bloodshot eyes looked hungover. Periodically, they'd hold their foreheads. When the third man said something they found amusing, they'd chuckle. Their clothes and hands were dirty, and their hair was matted and unwashed. Yet they seemed strangely comfortable in their surroundings.

My curiosity percolated, so I looked to either side for someone I could ask about the foursome. The buxom woman to my right seemed bored by the whole event. Her makeup was smeared and residue caked her face. She had her legs stretched out from a short skirt and dirty bare feet crossed at the ankles. A pair of four-inch stiletto heels rested in her lap.

I turned to her. "Excuse me?"

She looked at me like I'd landed from outer space.

"I was wondering about something."

"Yeah?" She seemed to be trying to figure out who or what I was.

"Those four people over there—the ones talking. They seem to know each other."

"So?"

"They don't seem unhappy to be here."

She shrugged. "Free meals."

"Do they come here a lot?"

"I've seen 'em a few times. Here. On the streets. Near the SAMM shelter."

"The homeless shelter? They're homeless, but they can go to SAMM and get free meals, help with detox and finding work, right?"

"Yeah. But they have to follow a bunch of rules. Follow a work schedule. Agree to detox. Go to counseling. All that crap."

"They'd have a place to sleep, food and people trying to help them."

"Some people don't want help. You have to want help before that stuff works." She gestured with her chin. "They'd rather sleep outside and take their chances on the street where they can get drugs and alcohol."

"Why would anybody sleep on cold pavement when they could sleep inside?"

"No drugs or alcohol are allowed inside SAMM. Outside, they can get whatever they want. They're frequent flyers."

"What?"

"That's what we call 'em. Frequent flyers. They run out of drug money and decide to get arrested a few days for free food and a shower. Or they pass out in front of somebody's business, the owner calls the cops to haul them away and they land here. They go before the judge, and he slaps them in jail. Sometimes they get so miserable, they're desperate to change their life and go to SAMM for help. But they have to want it." She shrugged. "I've been a flyer myself. A girl's got to make a living, but sometimes you need a break." She looked away.

Thirty-Seven

A voice boomed out, "Agatha Mundeen."

I stood. "Yes, sir?"

"The magistrate will see you." He unlocked the cell door, took me by the arm and led me down a corridor.

The courtroom wasn't large, but it was impressive. The round "State of Texas, Bexar County" seal loomed in front of the tall enclosure and stately chair where the judge would sit. The officer led me to a pew and sat me down. I looked around. There were four other arrestees, disheveled and handcuffed. Nobody else occupied the pews. No attorneys. No friends. No family members. Armed officers guarded doors to the courtroom.

The magistrate entered through drapes from behind the chair. He didn't look happy. The bailiff motioned us to stand. We clunked up, attempting to stand straight with our wrists bound.

"Bexar County Court, State of Texas, is now in session. The Honorable Magistrate Michael Ramirez presiding. You may be seated."

Robed, with steel-gray hair framing chiseled features, Ramirez looked daunting. He pulled a file in front of him, opened it and adjusted his glasses.

"State of Texas, Bexar County versus Agatha Emory Mundeen," the bailiff called.

An officer approached, lifted me by one arm and walked me toward the judge. I'd never felt so humiliated. The magistrate watched me approach without blinking.

"Agatha Emory Mundeen?"

"Yes, sir."

He proceeded to read me my rights. "Do you want a court-appointed lawyer to represent you?"

"No, sir. I hope to hire my own attorney."

"I see. You are charged with burglary." He paused. "Science laboratory at University of the Holy Trinity." He shook his head as though wondering why anybody would pull such a stunt. He flipped through the papers and scowled. He must have read I was found with a dead body. "How do you plead?"

"It was actually breaking and entering. I was searching for something, and I tripped on..."

He stared at me over his glasses. "You are charged with burglary. How do you plead?"

"Not guilty." If he wasn't going to let me explain, I was not going to plead guilty to being a thief.

"In view of the charge of burglary, which is a felony, I'm setting bond at ten thousand dollars. I order that you be remanded to the Bexar County Adult Detention Center."

"But, sir, I didn't..."

His gavel came down. Crack. "Next case."

Ten thousand dollars? I didn't have ten thousand dollars. Well, I did...in a CD at the bank. For emergencies. That I couldn't take out for a year. Meredith wouldn't have that much money. Or Sam either. I was going to a detention center? Was that jail?

I pictured myself behind bars. It was the last vision I remembered before I slumped to the floor.

The female officer waved smelling salts under my nose.

I turned away. "Stop. Stop..."

"Okay. Then take a deep breath."

I complied so she'd take the odor away. Blinking, I looked at her and looked around. I was sitting on the floor in an office outside the cell, still handcuffed.

She waited until I quit blinking and focused on her.
"How do you feel?"
"Lightheaded."
"Do you think you can stand?"
"I think so."
She helped me to my feet. "Are you ill?"
"I don't think so."
"You don't have any illness you know of?"
"No."
"All right. Looks like you just fainted. The magistrate said if you don't have a medical emergency, we can take you to jail. You'll get a medical evaluation there."

She escorted me back through the clerical area and stood with me by an exit door.

An officer by the door took my arm, led me through the door and stuffed me into a van with five other women. The seats had been removed to install metal benches that lined the sides of the vehicle. The officer behind me stepped into the van long enough to remove my handcuffs. I was rubbing both wrists when he grabbed my hand and handcuffed me to the woman beside me who smelled like she hadn't bathed in a month. He plopped me on the bench, backed out of the van and slid the door closed.

I looked around. We were caged like animals and linked like sausages. The females looked at me suspiciously. Nobody said anything. Only one looked halfway friendly. Another looked dazed from drugs. One tried to push away a snoring drunk woman leaning against her shoulder.

A see-though metal partition separated us from the driver. He probably wouldn't talk to us anyway.

Looking through barred windows on the other side of the van, I could see streaks in the sky but no daylight. The van's headlights lit the Frio Street sign and a street that mounded up to our left. Lights skittered across street signs: Buena Vista, W. Commerce, W. Travis; my first trip to San Antonio's west side.

The women started talking in low tones.

"What are you in for?"

"I had a bunch of outstanding parking tickets. You?"

"Assault. He had it coming."

"You back again, honey?" one said to the woman seated by her, who was slathered with makeup and wore fishnet stockings.

"Yeah. At least I'll get a good night's sleep." She yawned.

A tough-looking woman with crocodile eyes, handcuffed to a woman in a stupor, lifted her lids enough to stare at me with a dull expression. "You." She flipped her chin toward me. "What're you in for?"

"Murder." I hoped that would end the conversation. I had enough to worry about.

I turned my face away from the smelly creature attached to me and pondered how much more horrible my condition could become.

The woman who looked halfway friendly put a finger to her lips, then pointed around the ceiling of the van. The vehicle must be wired for sound in case we confessed to something on the way to jail.

Great. I'd just said I was arrested for murder. Everybody stopped talking.

When we turned left on W. Martin and onto Comal, the van slowed. We passed a multistory building on the right with a sign out front that read "Annex."

The building looming in front of us, five or six stories high, read: "Bexar County Sheriff's Office Adult Detention Center Facility." Our driver pulled around the side of the building and slowed.

Thirty-Eight

The van pulled into a garage that looked like a vault. There was no exit; only the entrance we came through. The van rolled to a stop, and a door behind it slid shut. The driver squawked into his radio. "Six females from magistrate in Sally Port."

In front of the van, a metal door glided open. A male and female officer emerged, approached our van and extracted us, one by one, while the driver watched. Their uniforms read "Bexar County Sheriff's Office."

"Is this jail?" I asked the woman.

She looked at me curiously. "Adult Detention. Booking," she said. "Yeah. Jail."

After checking to make sure we were handcuffed to each other, they herded us toward the cubicle they'd come from, a vestibule about six feet square. Officers nudged us inside and followed us into the enclosure. A door slid shut behind us.

I started sweating, feeling claustrophobic in the cramped space. The female officer started to pat down one of the women. She found a knife on her, confiscated it and handed it to another officer. Finished with her pat-down, she told the officer to apply leg iron restraints and remove her handcuffs.

Leg irons? Handcuffs were bad enough. Must be because the woman had a knife. Certainly they wouldn't...

She repeated her routine with the others. One had a bottle of pills and half a sandwich. Another had makeup in her pocket and a few dollars. She came toward the woman attached to my wrist and had to get close to frisk her. She wrinkled her nose, but her revulsion didn't make her search any less thorough. She clamped leg irons on her and removed the cuff from her wrist.

She came toward me. I was glad SAPD had taken my gloves, flashlight, dental pick and rope at UHT. It wouldn't look good to these officers, dressed in black like I was.

When she finished patting me down, I looked her square in the eyes. We were, after all, reasonable adults. "Surely you're not going to put me in leg irons. I was just in the wrong place looking for something and stumbled on..." Without a word, she snapped leg irons on my ankles and removed the handcuff from my wrist.

I had a horrible realization: everybody arrested—whether for unpaid parking tickets or murder—was treated exactly the same.

Mortified, I was close to hyperventilating. I was frantically rubbing my wrists so I wouldn't start crying. A door in front of us slid open.

The room before us was expansive and full of officers and arrestees. Officers behind a square configuration of counters walked from station to station inside the barricaded space, and talked to suspects in leg irons lined up outside the perimeter. More officers strolled through the room, surveying the proceedings.

The calendar on a counter showed Saturday, August 30, 1997. They hadn't changed it to Sunday. I was supposed to be enjoying the Labor Day holiday on Monday, Sept. 1st. and returning to class Tuesday. Instead, I might be booked into jail.

An officer stepped in front of us. "Incoming inmates form a line in front of desk number one."

Inmates? I was an inmate? I hadn't committed a crime—I'd simply tried to get information. They didn't even know my name or that I was a student or that I had been a bank executive. Or that I was terrified.

I shuffled with my van mates toward desk number one where two men were already lined up. Third in line, I took deep breaths to calm myself. I heard chains clanking. Down the hall to the left of the big room, an inmate in a short-sleeved red scrub suit, hands cuffed in front of him, dragged his feet attempting to walk. Metal chains secured his leg irons and handcuffs. An officer paced beside him. Would I have to share space with that man? My heart pounded. Door signs on cubicles to their right read "Attorney." Thank goodness Meredith was trying to find me a lawyer. My breathing slowed.

The interrogator finished with the first man. "Medical and banking," he called. Another officer led him away. I tried to overhear what the desk officer asked the next man. No such luck. When the questioner finished, he called, "Take him to clothing." Would I have to wear one of those jumpsuits?

He looked up at me. "Next."

I shuffled to the desk.

He took down my name, address, phone number, occupation, date of birth. Then he fingerprinted me.

"We'll send these to the state's AFIS database. Says here you collapsed at the magistrate's office."

"Yes, sir. I fainted."

"Do you feel normal now?"

Nothing about this was normal. "I feel all right, sir. I haven't eaten, which is probably why I fainted."

He studied me. "Your color looks okay. You'll get a sandwich and cookies in the holding cell. Have you ever been arrested?"

"No. Never."

"Do you have any medical or mental health needs?"

A splitting headache and being on the verge of hyperventilating probably didn't count. "No."

"You've never received mental health services?"

This might be my first time. "No."

"Do you have an emergency contact?"

I dared not give Sam's name. "Meredith Laughlin." I gave her address and phone number.

"Okay. Stand here for your photograph and ID card."

"I have an ID card with a photograph on my driver's license. The police took it."

"Okay. So you'll get another one." He clicked the camera. With my sour expression and smeared face, I probably looked like some loser on a wanted poster.

He motioned to a female officer. "Take her to holding."

"How long..." I started.

"Might be a while. We book sixty to eighty people on weekdays. This weekend, we'll have eighty to one hundred and twenty coming through intake. We'll call you. Next."

Thirty-Nine

The female officer took my elbow and steered me toward a side room partitioned with glass so booking officers could see inside. She nudged me through the door into a room three-quarters full of miserable-looking women. Rank body odors of every variety assaulted my nose. Hygiene wasn't a big consideration for people hauled to jail. I longed to shower and to escape to clean air.

Women crouched in corners or bunched in groups, trying to get as far away as they could from the entry door, like rats shying from light. Some looked sick and held their heads in their hands. From the stench, I thought several had been sick. Some had passed out against the wall. Others gazed into space, oblivious.

I moved gingerly toward the corner closest to the booking area and pretended I was invisible. A rotund woman sidled up.

"What you in here for, honey?" Her hair was stringy and her dark eyes were inscrutable. A cut oozed by the purple bruise on her temple.

"Burglary...maybe breaking and entering."

"B and E? That could be just trespass. No big deal. Burglary's worse. Is that why you're dressed in black with that stuff smeared on your face?"

I nodded.

"You don't look much like a burglar. This your first time?"

I nodded. She seemed to feel sorry for me—the first person to express a modicum of sympathy during this whole horrible ordeal. I felt my eyes mist.

"How about you?" I gurgled.

"I'm here for stealing. My husband beats me up." She pointed to bruises on her face. "He almost broke my arm. He was so drunk, he finally passed out. I called the cops to pick him up and took my kids to a cousin's farm out of town. Then I came back to town, stole something and made sure a cop saw it so I could get in here for protection. Real 'protective custody' inmates are charged with crimes against children or ex-gang members wanting protection. I just don't want to be at home when my husband gets out. The cops say they can't do nothin' unless he kills me. If I file charges, he'll be waiting when I get out and beat me up worse. At least I can sleep here and get a few meals and good showers. Get these cuts on my face doctored."

"Can't you run away? Go to a relative's house?"

"He knows the places I'd go to. I hope he doesn't remember that cousin's place out of town. If I'm in town, he'll find me."

"What if you go to another city...get a job?"

"Doin' what? I barely got out of sixth grade. Washin' dishes don't pay the rent."

"There must be something..."

"Yeah. Workin' the streets. Johns beat you up, too. And you got druggies and gangs to deal with."

"There's a battered women's shelter."

"Been thinkin' about that. I'd have to leave when he's working, which ain't very often, and take the kids. If he found us, he'd take it out on them. "

"I hear the shelter protects their clients."

"Yeah." She smirked. "If they can."

She didn't seem to have any other options. I wished I could help her.

I glanced around. "What crimes are people here for?"

"DUIs, drugs, child support, B and E, rape, murder. They've put the ones charged with murder someplace else."

"I saw a man shackled down the hall in a red suit. What do you think he did?" I asked.

"He's some kind of badass. They put 'em in red suits. Men in the general inmate population wear orange suits. He might've killed somebody. Could be a gang member, freaked out on drugs, be an out-of-control mental case or some kinda repeat criminal. They put him in cool-down for twenty-four hours. Then in lockdown. That's where all the gang members go."

"You sure know a lot about jail."

"I know a lot of people who've been in here. People talk."

A tough-looking woman sitting on the floor across the cell snapped menacing eyes on my companion.

"What's it like in lockdown?" I asked.

"It's got cells about six feet square. They lock 'em in twenty-three hours a day."

Being claustrophobic, I couldn't imagine it. "Must be horrible."

"And they don't know how long they'll be there. Could be twenty-four hours, could be a month. If they make trouble, it'll be longer. Sometimes they start yelling they can't breathe."

"From the shock of being confined?"

"Yeah. They can't see outside the cells. They yell, curse, bang the doors. Officers lift up peephole covers to see inside the cell and put food trays through slots in the door."

"Why would somebody do something to get themselves brought here and put into lockdown?"

She shrugged. "Bad choices. I'm Laney, by the way."

"Aggie." Guilty of bad choices.

Forty

A female officer called through the bars of our holding cell. "Mundeen!" I jumped three inches off the floor. Throaty laughs rumbled from around the room.

She motioned me to the door and pulled me into the booking area.

"Desk Number Three." She pointed. "Medical."

I shuffled toward the desk. Officer Michael McMullen confirmed my name and asked about my fainting at the magistrate's office.

"It was probably from lack of food." I didn't mention being angry and in a state of terror. "What if I get really sick?"

"You'll go to Medical at the annex."

"The annex?"

"All female inmates go there. It's across the street."

"I'll have a room...cell?"

"What are you charged with?"

"Burglary. You haven't read the police reports?"

"We don't get them. They go to the magistrate. We're a holding facility. You'll be housed at the annex in a large room like a dormitory—open bay unit."

"Does the annex have lockdown cells?"

"Twenty for women."

I swallowed, feeling shaky and feverish. "Who will see me if I'm sick?"

"University Health System docs from the medical school."

Everything was intertwined: the university, medical school, jail. It all depended on which route you took. How did I get so far off track? I held my forehead. How could I prove I didn't kill Eric Lager from here?

"You've never been in jail before, have you?"

I looked up with wet eyes. "No, sir."

"You get to make two free calls from booking."

"I called my friend from the magistrate's office."

"Okay. Then maybe you won't be here long."

"I could be a murder suspect." His eyes opened wider. "I was looking around in this lab, you see, because another man had died, and I was looking for clues. It was dark, and I tripped on him...the dead man."

He shook his head. "I thought I'd heard everything." He mumbled to himself. "Medium-high risk." He squinted up at me. "You gave your belongings to Banking?

"I didn't have anything. The police took everything."

My baby's bracelet was probably rotting on the campus lawn. While I rotted in jail.

A female officer took me back to the smelly holding cell.

"You can wait here until the van loads to go to the annex."

Laney was still there, slumped against the wall with her eyes closed. I slid down beside her.

"Laney, what's medium-high risk?"

"Anybody charged with a felony. Assault, sexual or otherwise. Battery, with or without a weapon. Burglary."

"Murder?"

"No. They put murder suspects in lockdown until they're convicted. Then they go to prison."

I shuddered.

Two officers entered our cell with bags of food. "Chow time," they said. My bag contained a sandwich and two cookies. I was starving. I inhaled the food and began to feel almost human.

The tough woman who'd given Laney a dirty look pulled her muscled body off the floor and swaggered over, tattooed arms swinging in full view. I stuffed the other cookie in my mouth before she could confiscate it.

"Back already, sweetie?" Her cold eyes bored through mine. "Where you goin'? Low-risk five-star hotel?" She sneered.

I hoped she wasn't going wherever I was going. When I didn't answer quickly enough, she narrowed her eyes and growled, "What are you in for?"

I swallowed my cookie and made my voice as deep as I could. "Murder."

Laney turned toward me, brows raised.

"Hmph," the toughie said. She shrugged, swaggered back to her space and slithered to the floor.

I put my hand in front of my mouth and whispered to Laney, "I didn't kill anybody. I thought that might make her leave us alone."

Laney covered the lower half of her face to hide her smile. "That ought to do it."

I must have dozed off. A crackling voice startled me awake.

"Anderson! Celaya! Jacoby! Mundeen!"

"That's us. Hurry up." Laney and I struggled to stand each other up and wobbled toward the door where the officer stood.

She pulled us out and pointed to the vestibule. "Van's waiting."

This was it, then. Meredith wasn't coming. Sam wasn't coming. No lawyer was asking to see me. Nobody was bailing me out. There was no way I could figure out who killed Kermit Carmody or Eric Lager. I'd been booked into jail.

Forty-One

Nobody talked on the short drive to the annex. I steeled myself for the next horrible event.

From the annex intake desk, they escorted us one by one to a clothing room.

The "clothing tech" inventoried our old clothes, looked for contraband and handed us blue scrub suits like the orange ones men wore at the main jail. I felt like an inmate.

Laney and I grabbed each other's hands for good luck. Then she shuffled off to her housing unit accompanied by an officer. Laney might be one of the few people happy to be here.

She looked back. "Laney Celaya," she said.

"Aggie Mundeen," I called, wondering if I'd ever see her again.

An officer escorted me to an elevator, up one floor and into a hall. In a large dormitory-like space, separated in the center by a Plexiglas wall, two dozen women meandered on each side of the partition.

Two-tiered bunks covered with army-like blankets were lined up in neat rows toward the rear. Metal tables with attached metal seats occupied the front of the rooms.

The center dividing wall ended at a half-circular surveillance room that backed up to the hall.

The officer inside, with her back to us, sealed off from both sections of the divided room, had a computer and extra screens to monitor every inch of both areas.

The inmates stopped to look at the new arrival in the hall. Me.

"You'll be on the right side," my escort said. "Medium-high risk."

The thought of milling among them terrified me. I thought I was going to faint.

The officer waited until I stabilized. If I acted like a wimp, I hated to think what might happen. I took a deep breath and nodded at her. She released my arm, and we entered the unit. Inmates closed around like predators stalking a kill. Some made comments under their breath.

She walked me to a bunk and pointed to the top tier. It was located second row back in the center. I counted bunks to either side. I didn't want to get into the wrong bed and give somebody an excuse to harass me. I hoped the occupant of the bottom bunk let me get up there.

"Shower over there behind the wall," she said. "Wash everything, including your hair. Inmates who don't stay clean are disciplined. Don't take all day."

Behind the wall were four shower heads with soap dispensers and enclosed toilets at one end. I chose a shower where I could see anybody coming before they got too close. It felt scrumptious scrubbing dirt from my hair and body and running my fingers through clean hair.

When I peered around the wall, the inmates were watching for me to come out—a fresh specimen. The officer, still there, looked around.

"No trouble here, understand? If the monitor sees anybody causing a problem, she'll send you straight to solitary."

Taking a deep breath, I straightened to my full five-foot-four height. Head high and eyes straight ahead, I walked toward my bunk with my heart skipping beats. When I was almost there, my protector walked toward the exit. Some eyes followed her; others stayed glued to me. The metal door banged shut.

As soon as she left, a tall, powerful-looking woman swaggered toward me, her swinging arms laced with tattoos—the same tough woman who'd confronted me in the holding cell.

"So. Here's our little murderer. You sure about that, cupcake? You don't look like you could kill nothin'."

I stood as straight as I could.

"I'm sure about that," I stated. "This time they think they've got me."

"This time? Whoo-eee. How 'bout that. You one badass. I smacked my man with a tire iron, but it didn't kill him. Too bad."

"Way to go, Thelma Louise," her friend called out. "Maybe next time."

"Yeah," she said. "Maybe next time. They nabbed me for assault and battery." She turned heel and jiggled a happy dance back to the table where her friends waited.

I exhaled and climbed up to my bunk, intending to stay there until they fed us. Incarceration was like being hospitalized, only we couldn't get better, go AWOL, or investigate the crime of which we were accused.

A young girl, fresh-scrubbed like me, came toward my perch.

"I'm on the bottom bunk. We're allowed to talk over there in the day room area." She walked toward the round metal tables and chairs.

She looked like a child. If she was brave enough to walk through the jungle, I could make it. I got down off the bunk, stood tall, looked straight ahead, walked toward the tables and sat.

"You don't look old enough to be here. What are you, eighteen?"

"Yes. They have cells for seventeen-year-olds who commit felonies."

"What did you do?"

"I needed money for food for my brothers. My parents are addicts. Most of the time they're too high to function or in jail. My brothers and I get so hungry. I thought if I had a bike, I could throw a paper route along with waiting tables, but..."

"You stole one. And the value of the bike made it a felony."

She hung her head. "I don't know what my brothers are going to do. They're eight and ten."

"Is there anybody to help them?"

"My aunt takes them home when she can and feeds them. But she has five kids of her own."

"Do you have a lawyer?"

"Court-appointed. He looked hungover when he came to see me."

"My friend's trying to get me a lawyer. Maybe he can help you. What's your name?"

"Sylvia Curtis." She told me her address, and I memorized it. This girl shouldn't have been here.

Forty-Two

We heard commotion near the ancient television set and moved closer to see what was happening.

"We're sorry to report a terrible tragedy," the newsman said. "Diana, Princess of Wales, was killed in an underground traffic tunnel in Paris this morning just after midnight. She and the man she was dating, Dodi Fayed, were involved in a high-speed chase, allegedly pursued by paparazzi, when the car they were in crashed into a tunnel wall. Diana was rushed to a hospital with massive head injuries, which led to her heart attack and death. Diana, Princess of Wales, is dead at age thirty-six."

We froze with shock.

I heard sniffles. As the station showed Diana's photographs, my fellow inmates started weeping. The more her death sank in, the more we cried.

"How could that happen?"

"She was so young."

"She was a true princess. How could she be dead?"

"She was so beautiful. So elegant. What will happen to her boys?"

The women would leave to wipe their faces and eyes, then return to the television, mesmerized by the unbelievably horrible tragedy.

Princess Diana was us. She was the little girl in each of us who played dress up in front of the mirror and dreamed of being a princess. Even the true Princess had suffered a catastrophe...like the unknown disaster we all feared.

I was no longer afraid of these women. We were Diana.

It grew quiet in Unit B. Women straggled to their bunks and cried, wrestling with Diana's tragedy and their own. I wanted to help them, but I had to get out of jail to do anything.

I heard clanking in the hall. A staffer and inmate rolled in food trays. After we'd finished our ten thirty a.m. lunch, an officer stuck her head in the door.

"Agatha Mundeen? You have a visitor."

She accompanied me to the first floor of the annex and led me to a waiting room.

Meredith sat there.

Forty-Three

I hugged her like she'd plucked me from a mine.

"How are you?" she asked. "It must be scary in here."

"It is, but it's better now. I guess you heard about Princess Diana?"

"Yes. Horrible. So tragic. But I do have good news. I found you a lawyer."

"You did? What's his name? How did you get him on Sunday?"

"His name is William Matheson. I scrolled defense attorneys in the yellow pages and caught him in his office doing paperwork. The best part is, when I told him your story, he said he thought he could get you out on bond. He seems very nice. He'll be here tomorrow."

I might be sprung. Tomorrow. "Did he say how much he charges?"

"It depends on what he has to do. Don't worry. I'll take care of it. You can pay me back."

"Okay. But *only* if I pay you back." I'd pay anything to get out of this place so I could investigate Eric Lager's murder. "What's going on around campus?"

"Not much, since it's Sunday. I cruised around the science building this morning before I came. SAPD stationed a police officer in front and in back of the building, but they're keeping a low profile. There's no crime scene tape. They're even letting people in to work in the lab. I parked discreetly on a side street from the building to see who went in."

"Perfect. Who did you see?"

"Those two guys from our class. The postdocs? They were in there about an hour. When they came out I decided to follow them."

My heart raced. "Did they take anything in or out?"

"They had backpacks. I couldn't tell."

"Did you see where they went?"

"I followed them in my car from a distance. They went all the way across campus to some fancy high-rise apartment building, the Garden Apartments. I think it's for visiting faculty."

"I know the place. Brandy lives there. Did they both go in?"

"Yes. And neither one of them came out."

They undoubtedly knew Brandy. Maybe in the Biblical sense. Maybe Bly lived there, Delay stayed with him rent-free, and they didn't want anybody to know.

"Did you see Brandy?"

"No."

"Meredith, since I'm stuck here, can you make a couple passes by those apartments and the lab this afternoon and maybe again tomorrow? University offices will be closed Labor Day weekend, but people will still be coming in and out of those apartments. They might even keep the lab open. SAPD might have requested it to watch who goes in. Since Brandy worked with Dr. Carmody, those postdocs might be involved with her. Somebody had it in for Dr. Carmody. It could have been them."

"I can't believe I'm about to do what Sam warns you not to do."

"Just don't get yourself jailed. It really inhibits progress."

Forty-Four

I was back in my bunk, thinking how Brandy and the postdocs could have conspired to bump off Carmody. They could be doing experiments and evaluating data that Brandy couldn't carry out alone without arousing suspicion. They'd know enough about Carmody's research to steal his ideas. But first they'd have to kill him. When Eric Lager realized what they were doing, they could have killed him too. How was I going to prove that?

I was dozing off when Thelma Louise bellowed, "It's four thirty, chil'en. Middle of the afternoon. Great time for dinner, ain't it?"

Inmates circled the cart. We were pretty hungry from pouring out grief over Diana. After dinner, everybody meandered toward the TV.

Henri Paul, head of security at the Ritz, had driven the Mercedes that crashed. It was rumored he'd been drinking. Dodi and Paul died at the scene. Diana survived the crash but died at the hospital at four a.m. Diana and Dodi's bodyguard, Trevor Rees-Jones, the only survivor, suffered serious head injuries. A few careless moments. Then disaster. I'd begun to understand how tragedy occurred.

Thelma Louise piped up. "Nobody's goin' to talk about Leroy when he kicks the bucket. Unless it's about the bad things he done."

They giggled, then grew sad and straggled to their bunks. There was nothing else to do but eat, sleep, grieve and worry. I crawled on my bunk, threw an arm over my eyes to block the florescent lights and thought about my predicament. And about Sam. *I'd give anything if you hadn't done this*, he said. *But you did.* Those words hurt the most. I'd gotten myself into a mess that even Sam couldn't undo. He was already provoked by my curiosity and interference. This time, I might have pushed him beyond his ability to forgive.

Forty-Five

The door to Unit B clanged open.

"You've got another visitor, Mundeen."

I clamored down from the bunk. With jealous eyes flipping toward me, I slithered toward the door fast as I could.

"Just a relative," I said over my shoulder. "She's lonely. Has to work tomorrow on Labor Day."

We rode in silence to the first floor. It couldn't be the attorney this late on Sunday afternoon. Had Meredith discovered something?

I hustled toward the visitors' area. She was there, smirking.

"You went back to campus. What did you see?"

"I saw Brandy huddling with one of the postdocs as they came out of the lab. They were having an intense conversation. They crossed over the street, away from the lab, chattering like chipmunks. When they got under a tree, they high-fived. Then he mashed her up against the trunk and kissed her. He ran his hands all over her and under her clothes. I thought he might actually undress her until a car rumbled by. Then they laughed and started walking across campus."

"What did he look like? Did he have a big nose?"

"No. Just average."

"Must be Stanley Bly. He lives in those Garden Apartments, same as Brandy."

I knew from the reverse directory that Bly was the one paying rent. It apparently didn't take him long to strike up an intimate friendship with Brandy. I wasn't sure where Phillip-Delay-with-the-nose fit in.

"Okay," I said. "The postdocs and Brandy have access to the lab and are familiar with Dr. Carmody's and Eric Lager's work. Interesting, don't you think? Great work, Meredith. Don't tell Sam."

"Don't worry. You'll have to tell him yourself, Aggie. And when you get out, don't do anything to get yourself back in here."

"I hear you. Don't worry."

The officer led me back to Unit B.

Excited by the news, I crawled into my bunk and drifted in and out of a fitful sleep. I'd finally relaxed into oblivion when somebody turned on painfully white overhead lights and shouted, "Breakfast. Rise and shine." I tried to shade my eyes enough to open them.

"It feels like the middle of the night," I said to nobody.

"It *is* the middle of the night. It's three a.m."

"Breakfast?" They couldn't be serious. This was sleep-deprivation torture. Wasn't that illegal?

"Yeah. You'd better eat it. It's a long time until lunch."

After I finished, I made my way back to my penthouse, planning to crawl up there, put my arms over my face and sleep until a decent hour.

When I heard water running, I came to my senses. Bath time. I needed to get up and take a bath. My attorney was coming to see me today. It was Monday, September first. Labor Day. I had to be ready.

By the time I bathed, washed my hair and fluffed it as best I could, it was time for lunch: ten thirty a.m. Just as we finished, an officer came to the door, stuck her head in and beckoned me.

"You have a visitor." She accompanied me to the first floor of the annex and put me into a transport van. The driver headed for the main jail.

Forty-Six

The officer who received me at booking led me down the hall past doors marked "Attorney" and swung right to an area that ended behind cubicles.

"Your attorney wants to talk to you. Sit here." She pointed to the round stool in one of the partitioned booths. "Pick up the receiver." My heart pumped with anticipation.

Through the glass, I saw a rotund man with a paunch descend in front of my line of vision. His long-sleeved shirt closed at the top with a string tie too flimsy for his bulging neck. His face and hair were reddish, probably from the heat. Or from alcohol. He removed his white Stetson, revealing a low part to one side. From the line of demarcation, thin hair swept across his shiny head. His eyes, deep-set and direct, evaluated me.

"Your friend, Meredith Laughlin, asked me to come see you." Since we couldn't shake hands, he raised a finger in salute. "S. William Matheson the third, Attorney at Law."

"Thank you for coming. I'm Agatha Mundeen. Friends call me Aggie."

"Let's hope I fall into that category. I've read your file. Want to tell me what happened?"

He leaned back and folded his arms while I went through events leading to my arrest.

He listened, studying me intently, and interrupted a few times. Why was I in the lab? What did I hope to find? Had I taken anything? Why didn't I just let police handle the investigation about Dr. Carmody? That was a hard question to answer, but I tried to explain.

What did Eric Lager look like when I found him on the floor? Were there signs anyone else had recently been in the lab? Had I touched the spray bottle near Eric?

Each time I answered, he studied me, watching when I gestured or changed the position of my body.

I sensed he was taking my measure as much as considering my answers.

He pursed his lips and looked through the file again. "Have you been interviewed for PR, a personal recognizance bond?"

"Nobody mentioned that. After I fainted in the courtroom, the magistrate told the officer I could be medically evaluated here."

"I see. I understand you're a student." He looked skeptical. "Do you have a job?"

"I was vice president of a bank in Chicago before I moved here. Now I'm a liberal arts graduate student studying how to avoid aging."

He threw his head back and guffawed. "Let me know how that goes."

"I write the column 'Stay Young with Aggie.'"

"I see. Have you owned a house here more than a year?"

"Yes."

"Have you ever been arrested?"

"No. Never. I haven't even had a parking ticket in twenty years."

"Do you have any relatives here?"

"No, sir. My family all died. But I have friends here, Meredith Laughlin, my two neighbors on either side, and Detective Sam Vanderhoven."

"Vanderhoven is a friend of yours?"

"Yes."

"Hmm. That so. Well, I've discussed this with your friend Ms. Laughlin, and I'm going to stick my neck out here. I believe your story—strange though it is. I don't believe you killed anybody or that you're a flight risk. You might make a pretty good witness, if it comes to that."

"No, sir. I mean, yes, sir."

"I'm going to post an attorney's bond." He held up some papers. "That means I'm going to fill out these papers guaranteeing that you'll appear before the district judge for trial. To guarantee your appearance, I have to swear I have at least twenty thousand dollars equity in my home. If you don't show up for trial, the court puts a lien on my house."

"Don't worry, Mr. Matheson. I'd never put you in that position."

"Good. I can't afford it. I'm charging Ms. Laughlin a higher fee than usual because I'm posting this bond. Financial matters will be between you and her."

"Yes, sir. Does that mean I can get out of jail?"

"Yes. As soon as they process these papers." He started writing.

I started getting curious. Why would a complete stranger take a risk on me? How much was Meredith paying this man?

"Do you represent a lot of criminals?"

"Too many. I used to work in the DA's office. Felt sorry for some of the poor bastards we prosecuted." He looked up. "Sorry. For the language and all." He looked back at the papers. "I thought I ought to help them. Most of them didn't have anybody else to do it."

Where had his empathy come from? Maybe he'd been the black sheep in his family. Had felt downtrodden. I noticed my curiosity hadn't died.

He finished writing. "Okay. I'm going to hand over fifteen dollars to the clerk to process these release papers. They'll take you back to the annex to get your clothes and belongings." He looked at his Seiko. "One o'clock. Normally, they'd hold you overnight and release you in the morning. But they'll try to get you out this afternoon so they can join their families for the rest of Labor Day. When they call me, I'll wait for you at the front of the main jail."

I was going to get out of jail! He'd done it, this fat, balding, perfect angel. I'd have hugged him if I could get to him. And Meredith had found him, bless her heart.

"There's two women I need to tell you about," I called to his back. "Laney Celaya and Sylvia Curtis."

I wasn't sure he heard me about Laney and Sylvia. When the officer took my arm, a smile played around her lips. The back of Matheson's shirt, stuck to his skin, disappeared from my view.

Forty-Seven

An officer put me back into the van, handcuffed and alone. The driver headed back toward the annex.

The intake officer gave me a onceover. "You'll be released on an attorney's bond. That's unusual. Officer Melton will take you up to Unit B to get your bedding. When you get back here, we'll get your clothes out of the property room."

So much for a warm send-off. Officer Melton escorted me back to Unit B and stood while I stripped my bunk. I was shaky climbing down.

Sylvia Curtis came over. "How'd it go?"

"It was okay. The attorney asked me questions, trying to prepare me for trial. They said to bring my stuff downstairs in case he could get me out on bond." I couldn't bring myself to tell her I'd be released.

After the others wandered off, I whispered to Sylvia. "I gave him your name. I'll tell him about you, but can't promise anything."

She squeezed my arm and smiled.

Thelma Louise said, "A squeaky-clean burglar and killer."

We all giggled. As I started to follow the officer out the door, Sylvia grasped my hand. Others gestured with small waves as I walked through them.

"Don't come back, Aggie."

When we got to the annex booking area, the tech brought a bag with my black break-in clothes, wadded up and unwashed, from the property room. I peered inside the bag.

"Did you see a baby's bracelet anywhere? Pink with lettering on it?"

She shook her head. "What you wore in is all we have." I changed in a small room. It was good to be back in my own clothes, even though they weren't clean.

Officer Melton accompanied me in the van to the main jail and booking desk.

"Agatha Mundeen. She's here to be released."

"Put her in holding while we wait on the papers."

This holding cell was different from the smelly one. I slid down the wall, leaned against it and closed my eyes, hoping S. William Matheson III didn't renege on his plan when he saw me dressed in black burglar attire.

I dozed off and dreamed about being called to the podium to accept a journalism prize for my comprehensive newspaper series explaining current discoveries on extending human life and health. Why did the voice announcing me sound so harsh?

"Agatha Mundeen! Get up and come over here."

I shook myself awake, stood and walked toward the officer. While she unlocked the door, I noticed the booking area looked different. Friendlier. More efficient. S. William Matheson III lumbered up from a chair and met me at the main desk. I signed release papers, and he led me to his car.

Even the heat felt good. I inhaled deep breaths of free air. When he opened the passenger door to the front seat, I felt like Princess Diana gliding into my limousine.

I studied every person, tree, bush and building on the way to my Burr Road house. I told Mr. Matheson all I knew about Laney Celaya and Sylvia Curtis and asked for a pencil and paper to write down Sylvia's address. He said he'd get Laney's address from the detention center's records.

"They don't have any money," I said, "but I'll pay you if you can help them." I'd have to reimburse Meredith first and hope Matheson didn't bankrupt me.

"I'll see what I can do."

When he cruised up the hill to my house, we passed Sam's unmarked car parked at the curb four houses before mine. I stared briefly. When I sensed Matheson had seen me gawk, I looked away.

"Friend of yours?"

"I just thought it was somebody I knew."

Forty-Eight

I heard Sam start his car and follow us to my curb. When Matheson accompanied me to my door, Sam strode up the driveway. He stood there, hands in his pockets, until Matheson acknowledged his presence.

"Is there a problem, Officer?" Matheson said. He recognized Sam, even in plainclothes.

"No problem, Counselor. She's a friend. I heard she was being released."

Defense lawyers and cops don't hold each other in high regard. Policemen think defense attorneys play for the wrong team. Officers go to a lot of trouble to arrest bad guys and get them off the streets, and defense lawyers try to slip them out of jail. Not a strong basis for friendship.

"I'm her defense lawyer. I hope I won't be sorry."

"You should be all right," Sam said. He was all business with S. William Matheson III. I couldn't tell whether that was a ruse to let the attorney know he hadn't been involved in my case, or whether his detached demeanor signaled his permanent future attitude toward me.

I was, after all, an ex-jailbird.

"I guess you can get into the house?" Matheson said.

I nodded.

"I'll call you later," he said. "Officer." He tipped his Stetson to Sam and walked toward his car.

"Thank you, Mr. Matheson, for everything," I called.

We watched him until he pulled away from the curb. Then we turned and walked to my door.

"Matheson's an okay guy."

"He posted bond for me. I hope I can scrape together enough to pay him."

"Do you have a key hidden to get in?"

"I have a house key in the flower beds and car keys in the house."

I counted shrubs planted to the left of my front door stoop. Stepping behind the third bush, I knelt down, measured a thumb-to-index finger span behind the base of a plant and started digging. My house key was three inches down in the dirt. When I finished, the knees of my black break-in pants were covered with dirt, and my hands and nails were grubby. I brushed off my pants, shook dirt off my hands and wiped off the key. I was so grateful to be back at my house that just turning the key in the lock almost made me cry. I opened the door, saw the living room and bawled.

The magnificent square wood table between my sofas was upended. My prize Tabriz rug underneath had been rolled up and shoved aside. My sofa pillows were scattered and thrown on the floor. The antique cabinet I'd captured at Broadway Antique Auction had its lower drawers wrenched open. The open space at the top held my CD player, but somebody had turned the player sideways to search behind it. My CDs were scattered, not lined up by types of music.

I ran crying into my kitchen. Upper cabinets were open with only a few dishes left inside so someone could run a hand across the back of every shelf. Dishes were strewn across countertops. Drawers gaped open, their cutlery, placemats and napkins slung out. Cabinet doors under the sink hung open, with cleaning supplies ejected to the floor, and the plumbing fixture elbow hanging in a void.

Expecting the worst, I made myself go to the bedroom. Every inch had been searched and jumbled. With Sam plodding down the hall behind me, I ran first to the fake, hollowed-out book in the case on the far wall. He stopped at the bedroom door. My back was toward him.

I reached for *An In-Depth History of the World,* the tome that looked like it had a thousand pages where I hid my baby's hospital bracelet. The tiny pink, plastic circle had the words, "Lee Mary Mundeen. Girl. 7 lbs. 4 oz. 16 inches. Mother: Agatha Emory Mundeen."

The amulet wasn't inside the fake book. I thought I'd lost it somewhere on campus when I broke into the lab, but I had to look. Lee's bracelet was my talisman—my good luck charm. I'd lost it before but had always retrieved it. To keep me safe, I'd worn it to campus that night. Now it was gone for good.

Drawers were yanked out, clothes rifled, ripped off hangers and tossed with shoes on the floor. Sam stood in the doorframe, silent.

In the bathroom, cabinets and drawers gaped open with toiletries and linens strewn around. I grabbed two tissues, slogged back to the living room, replaced the cushions on one sofa and sank down. Sam came and sat on the other end, stiff and expressionless.

"Who would have done this? What kind of thief would break into this ordinary house? It doesn't look like they took anything. There wasn't anything to take. They just messed everything up." I sniffed. I'd been violated and humiliated so many times. And now this.

"How could they break in here without my neighbors Grace or Anna hearing the commotion and calling the police?" I blew my nose.

"I don't think it was robbery, Aggie. The police came to search your house."

Of course they did. I was a murder suspect. But I was still angry.

"You let them do that?"

"I didn't have anything to say about it. I wasn't even on the case, remember?"

I stopped to sniff and think and wipe my eyes.

"What were they looking for?"

"Probably a nasal spray bottle like the one they found near Eric Lager. Or some substance you could have put in it. Maybe they wanted to compare your fingerprints with prints on that bottle."

I raised my chin and froze him with a haughty glare.

"Well, they didn't find any of that. I didn't kill Eric Lager. How many times do I have to tell you that?" I started blubbering again.

He pushed up off the couch, walked over, sat beside me and put his arm around my shoulders.

"I know you didn't kill Eric Lager. But you were there. The police have to follow through with their investigation."

"I know." I wiped my eyes again and rubbed a tissue under my nose before I rested my head on his shoulder. "It's so horrible to be handcuffed and have locks on your ankles so you can barely walk and be patted down all the time. Like a common criminal." My tears started flowing.

"I know."

"And you never know where they're taking you. And nobody ever believes you. And you can't even talk to the judge because he won't listen."

"I know."

"And when you're taken to jail those women smell so bad. They could be murderers and thieves and on drugs, and you're right in the middle of them."

"I know."

"And then, in jail, they dump you some place you can't even imagine. They put you in a room with all these women milling around, and you don't know what they've done or what they'll do to you." I turned my face into his shoulder and wept.

He kept patting my back. "I know. I know."

When I finally wound down and backed away, I saw I'd really soaked his shirt. I touched it. "I'm sorry."

"It's okay. I've been meaning to get a new one."

"I'd better go freshen up."

"Okay."

I closed the door to my bedroom, took a shower and washed my face and hair. I felt so much cleaner using my own bathroom. I put on clean underwear, slacks, deodorant, a fresh top and even a little makeup. I didn't want to take too long because I was afraid Sam would leave. I felt safe with him there.

When I returned to the living room, he'd replaced the sofa cushions, rolled out the rug, placed my coffee table on top and was staring into the drawer of my antique cabinet.

"I thought you might want to do your own rearranging," he said. He turned, stopped and looked me up and down. "You look like my Aggie again."

He walked toward me, arms outstretched, and I fell into them.

Forty-Nine

We stood there, grasping each other. This moment could so easily have been lost. When he released me and looked into my eyes, I saw worry and confusion and affection. Or was it love? Whatever it was, he wiped my eyes. Then he kissed me.

It was a lingering kiss, and when he pulled me to him and wrapped his arms around me, I realized how soggy his shirt was. I thought about telling him if he wanted to take it off, I could wash it.

That probably wasn't a good idea. Not now. Not after what I'd been through. He must have been under stress too. Trying to learn details about the crime scene without implicating himself. Worrying about what was happening to me in jail. We had a lot to catch up on and mountains in front of us.

When we made love, and I thought we would eventually, I wanted everything to be perfect, with no worries, no secrets, no looming questions. I wanted to be in a place where I could concentrate on Sam. Just Sam. This was not the time to offer to wash his shirt.

I pulled slowly away, took his hand and led him to the couch. "I need you to tell me what happened while I was in jail." He sighed, leaned back against the cushions and stretched both hands behind his head.

"Well, the young officer on the campus lawn apparently wasn't concerned that I showed up. She's been out on patrol and I've been in the office with homicide detectives, so I never saw her after that night. The homicide guys knew you were my friend. Your name came up when Carmody died, so they knew I couldn't get involved in the Lager case. When they talked about it, they'd talk freely and act like I wasn't there. If I had a question, I'd ask it one on one, and the guy knew enough not to blab."

I smiled.

"One guy was rushing out the door to a crime scene at the end of the day," he said, "and he asked me to file a report for him. What he gave me were police reports about Eric Lager's murder. I flipped through them and filed them in the appropriate cabinet. So I knew everything they knew."

"There was fungus in Eric Lager's nasal spray?"

"That's what they think. There were no trauma marks, no signs of a struggle, no fingerprints in the lab except those of people who were supposed to be there...students, teachers, professors. They checked out most of those prints after Carmody died, but they have a few more to check. They requested a rush on the autopsy and toxicology reports. We should have those back in a couple of days."

"Our class is supposed to meet twice this week as usual, starting tomorrow."

He looked incredulous. "And you want to go back?"

"I want to learn how genes affect aging. Dr. Bigsby will probably teach the class."

"I'm sure everybody over there knows Eric Lager was killed, Aggie. It's been in the papers. And they probably know you were jailed as a suspect, or at least as a burglar, for breaking into the lab. Aren't you embarrassed about that?"

"Well, yes, but since I had a good reason to break in, and I didn't kill him, I know they'll eventually learn the truth."

"You understand the killer is still out there and that it might be someone in class."

"Yes. Exactly. If I'm back in class, they'll know I didn't kill Eric Lager. I'll announce it."

"You'll announce it. In class. You're not the least bit worried about being back on that campus?"

"Not in broad daylight. There are people all over the place."

"And you absolutely will *not* go back into that lab."

"That probably wouldn't be wise."

"That's an understatement. If the killer sees you're out of jail and thinks you're no longer a suspect, he'll realize he's still at risk."

"Exactly."

"He won't know if the police found Eric's spray bottle. The killer probably left fast and dropped it. He might think you picked it up. And he'll be desperate to get it back."

"In the middle of campus, in the middle of the day, what could anybody possibly do to me?"

"Accost you on campus when nobody else is around. Threaten you. Spray that deadly stuff in your nose. Follow you home and do it later...I'd better station a cop near your house."

"I promise I won't let anybody get that close to me, on campus or here. I'll carry pepper spray." I had no idea where to get pepper spray. "If I don't go back, the killer will think he got away with murder and won't do anything. My being at the university, released from jail, will make the killer realize he has to *do* something. SAPD can put plainclothes cops on campus. When the killer makes a move, your guys will be there to catch him."

He shook his head. "I can't disagree with your logic. But I can't put you in jeopardy."

I thought I was in greater jeopardy if I didn't flush out the killer. I stiffened my back and adopted my most stern look.

"I have every right to go back. It's a free country, and I'm not in custody."

"Why can't you just be scared, like normal people? Why do you have to be so meddlesome? And so damned logical?"

"I'll take that as a compliment."

He sighed. I think he was afraid I might go back, no matter what he said, and he'd better figure out a way to protect me.

"Maybe you could wear a wire. A cop could tail you. If anybody even gets close, you call for help, and the cop is right there."

I mentally smiled. What I actually did was look thoughtfully at the ceiling.

"That might work."

"I need to think about this," he said. "Don't plan to go back on campus tomorrow unless we talk first. I'm going to see if there's new information at the office. Lock the doors after me and don't go anywhere."

"I've got to get groceries. I'll go visit Grace. Maybe she'll take me."

"Don't go anywhere alone. And be very alert about who's around you."

I nodded.

He left, looking tired and worried.

You look like my Aggie again, he had said. *My Aggie...*

I liked the sound of that.

Fifty

I called Meredith. "How can I ever thank you for finding me a lawyer?"

"Aggie, you're home! Thank goodness. What did you think of him?"

"I think you sent me an angel. It would be hard not to like somebody who gets you out of jail. I think he believed me. And I'm going to repay you. How much did you pay him?"

"Two thousand dollars up front. If he decided to post bond after talking to you, I signed a paper saying I'd owe him twenty thousand dollars if you didn't show up for your court hearing."

"You know I'll show up. And I'll pay you whatever he charges."

If I could attend class and flush out the killer, I'd be exonerated and there would be no need for a trial. I wasn't ready to divulge details to Meredith, especially since I didn't know yet what they were.

"Sam thinks it might be all right for me to attend class tomorrow, if I promise not to go back to the lab."

"Certainly not to the lab. Class should be okay. I'll be with you, along with all the others."

"Yes. And Sam will have plainclothes cops on campus."

I found a cold Diet Dr. Pepper and dried-out cheese in the refrigerator. Better than nothing. My peanut butter jar in the pantry was almost empty. I managed to scrape out a tablespoon and drop a glob of grape jelly on top. Fortified, I called my neighbor Grace.

"Hi, Grace. It's me."

"Aggie. I saw you go inside and hoped you'd call. Are you all right? I mean, after being..."

"It's okay to say it. In jail. I was in jail."

"I knew about it because the police came by and were swarming inside your house. I stomped over there and demanded to know what they were doing. They were making a mess, and I couldn't stop them. They kept me busy asking questions about you."

"It's okay. The house isn't too bad. It's just a matter of straightening up. They were just doing their job. Are you busy? Can I come over?"

"Sure. We can talk while I finish grouting this table."

"I'll be over in ten minutes."

I cradled the phone and peered through the glass in the top half of my back door. My small backyard was rife with weeds and dead St. Augustine grass, a common late-summer condition. Having been busy studying, attending class, sleuthing and going to jail, I'd neglected my yard more than usual.

When cool weather revived us in mid-October, I'd have to get busy. There were no signs of footprints outside, even though the police had been there. Indentations are hard to make in cracked, dry earth.

The kitchen door that led to the garage was locked, so I didn't bother to go in there.

Sam and Meredith had driven my car home. SAPD had undoubtedly searched Albatross. I knew the garage door to the driveway was locked because Sam had checked it.

After inspecting my bedroom and bathroom windows to make sure they were secure and connected to the alarm, I felt pretty safe. I'd had the system installed after somebody tried to break into my house last semester when I was inside studying. If I hadn't screamed, they'd have broken in.

I put on tennis shoes in case Grace's mutt, Boffo, decided to pounce on my feet. Even though I'd previously befriended him with doggy treats, I wasn't sure he'd remember.

Padding back to the living room, I peeked through the blinds. My front yard looked undisturbed. No parked cars lurked in either direction down Burr Road. The green expanse of lawn across the street in Ft. Sam Houston comforted me. I was ready to visit Grace.

I slipped off the door chain, stepped onto my front stoop and eased onto round stones that led to the asphalt driveway by her yard. The heat was stifling, but it felt glorious being outside. When I knocked on Grace's door, Boffo started barking.

She opened the door. "Come in, come in," she bubbled.

She held a grout-smeared rubber glove in one hand. If she hadn't looked so sticky, I'd have hugged her. More white strands than I remembered poked out from the gray hair she tried unsuccessfully to capture in a bun. In her sixties, her face was pink and young with the excitement of enjoying life.

Boffo stood growling, frozen to his spot, looking from my face to my shoes. His terrier/dachshund brain apparently wavered between greeting a friend and attacking my tennis shoes. Grace once entered him in Earthdog competitions where he chased rats through tunnels and routed them out. He'd done pretty well but had trouble distinguishing prey from feet. He was probably nearsighted. We were once pretty chummy, but we hadn't bonded in a while.

One of Grace's tile tables occupied a place of honor in her living room. She'd designed a gray tile dove surrounded by lighter and lighter tiles.

"I see you finished your dove. Beautiful."

"That one gives me peace every time I walk by." Surviving tragedies in her life had made Grace wise. I loved the way she relished every moment of her existence.

"Come into the kitchen," she said. "I'm grouting."

"Do you have doggy treats?"

"You bet."

She pointed to treats on a countertop. I grabbed the bag and offered him one.

He chewed, his tale wagging. I knew I could handle Boffo. When I gave him a second treat and petted the back of his head, he looked up gratefully, burped and curled up on the floor near my shoes.

In the middle of Grace's kitchen, a round wrought-iron table stood on newspapers. She was tiling the top with random shapes of colorful tiles in orange, red, fuchsia, and yellow.

I smiled. "This one must be for your patio."

"Yes, it's the dining table. I'll use variations of the same colors to make side tables for the sofa. I'll probably do something different for tables by the other chairs."

People like Grace were the reason scientists should manipulate genes to extend lifespans. She would be nurturing people and creating beauty until she ceased to exist on the Earth.

She pulled on her other glove, grabbed her trowel, scooped up fresh grout and pressed it between tiles on her table.

"You must teach me how to do that," I said.

"If you stop taking classes long enough, I will." She grinned, then looked up with a serious expression. "I've been reading about your professors—the two who died."

"Yes. Both murdered. It's horrible. The police thought I killed the second one. That's why I was in jail."

"You? That's preposterous."

"Well, I broke into the science lab to look for clues to the first professor's murder, bumped into the second man's body and they found me."

"I guess that didn't look good."

"No."

"That's why they were pawing through your house? To find something to tie you to his murder?"

"Yes. There was a bottle of nasal spray near him. They think something inside the bottle killed him."

"Be careful where you buy your cold remedies, right?"

"The killer must have added something to the spray. They'll know what the substance was when they get the autopsy and toxicology reports. Whatever it was, I don't have any of it, so that should clear me as a suspect. I didn't particularly like those professors, although I learned Dr. Carmody did have a soft side. But I had no motive for killing them. A fungus growing in Dr. Carmody's nasal spray killed him."

"Hmm. Nasal sprays are so common. Half the people in San Antonio have allergies."

"Exactly. And since Dr. Carmody was famous for researching genes that affect aging, somebody probably killed him for what he knew."

"And the other man?"

"The killer probably thought he discovered Carmody's secret."

"Somebody on that campus has gone crazy. I bet your detective friend wants you to stay away from there."

"Actually, Sam just got through telling me not to return. That's why I need to talk to you. You give such thoughtful advice."

"Uh-oh. I see where this is going." She pressed the last grout between tiles, peeled off her gloves and dumped them into a bucket of water. I knew we had a few minutes to wait while the grout between tiles hardened enough so she could wipe off the excess. "Why in the world," she said, "would you want to go back to this school when two murders were committed there?"

Why indeed? I lined up points of argument in my head. Grace was smart and logical. If I could convince her, I'd have a barrage of plausible reasons ready to use on Sam. I wasn't about to be humiliated and jailed for something I didn't do and then let the whole mess drop and hope that somebody solved it.

She wet a sponge to clean excess grout off the tiles and bent over her table. I was glad she was occupied while she listened to my reasoning.

"First of all, classes will go on as usual. UHT will try to maintain normalcy on campus so there's no uproar and everybody can continue with their education. Tuition is really high at this school. They don't want the issue of refunds added to a discussion of two deaths."

"Okay. What does that have to do with you?"

"Everybody at UHT thinks I'm in jail. If the killer thinks he's off scot-free, he or she won't have to do a thing. The killer is obviously a person who visits the lab on a regular basis. Everybody is used to seeing this person there. It must be a scientist who knows what to look for and will wait for the right opportunity to revisit the lab. When the timing is right, he'll return to the lab for some logical reason, memorize or copy Carmody and Eric's work, make sure the premises appear undisturbed and take the knowledge back to his own facility. He'll wait patiently until the furor is over. Once the murder cases grow cold, the thief and colleagues will surprisingly unearth a breakthrough. It will be different enough from the work at UHT's lab so that nobody makes the connection with their new discovery."

She had wiped the tiles clean. Their brilliance emerged.

"Your table is going to be spectacular."

"Yes. It's looking good. Now. Why do *you* have go back there?"

"If I'm back in school, I upset the killer's plan. The murderer thinks I'm no longer a suspect. If I were, I'd still be in jail. The killer will wonder if I turned in the nasal spray, or if the police have it and matched the killer's fingerprints to the bottle. Police probably already have the culprit's fingerprints from checking lab visitors after Carmody's murder. But the killer doesn't know that. With me out of jail, he's forced to act. He has to hurry and obtain secrets about genes that Carmody and Eric discovered and abscond with the information before the police get on his trail. The cops are watching all the scientists associated with the lab. When one makes a move, they'll close in."

"Your return to class will trigger the killer to act. You're acting as bait."

"Exactly."

"What if the killer decides *you* have the nasal spray bottle? And he has to get it from you before police find his prints on it?

What if he can't find any notes about the discovery and thinks you stole them?"

"Sam and I talked about that. He'll keep a tail on me and a plainclothes cop nearby on campus. And I'll have pepper spray."

"Where are you going to get that?"

"I don't know yet. Maybe the drugstore."

"What if the killer follows you home?"

"Sam will have a cop outside here. And I took a self-defense class."

She wasn't impressed. "I know the police are skilled, Aggie, but there's always a chance the killer gets to you before they can. I'd hate for you to get hurt."

"I'd hate it too. Sam debated having me wear a wire to record what the killer says if he accosts me. But I'm afraid if the murderer finds me wired, he'll become instantly more violent and dangerous."

"I'd be afraid of that too."

We lapsed into silence while she rinsed her sponge and polished tiles.

There had to be a way for me to flush out this killer and feel protected. The killer wouldn't want to hurt me until he had the spray bottle in his possession. I started considering options.

"Aggie," Grace said. "You need to think about this a long time before you go back to campus."

"I know. But I don't have any food. Can you drive me to Whole Foods?"

Fifty-One

I liked to shop at Whole Foods when I wanted something special. After jail food, I longed for gourmet goodies.

Grace washed goop off her hands.

"Do you have a floppy hat?" I asked her. "I'd prefer not to be recognized yet."

"I have a battered fishing cap you can pull down. Used to belong to Charlie, my first husband."

"That'll be fine. Especially with my sunglasses."

We piled into her red 1990 Honda Civic Wagon. Her garage was attached, like mine, so we entered it from her kitchen. I crunched the hat down and slid low in the seat, in case somebody was watching cars leave from our area. Grace's bright red vehicle was hard to miss. It was approaching clunker stage but had only seventy thousand miles. She and the car might well last forever. Grace liked it because she could pile boxes of tiles and sacks of grout behind the backseat. Every time we hit a bump, I heard tiles crash together and crack into shards. That was one way to get intriguing designs.

Alamo Quarry Market was pretty busy on Labor Day with people shopping for the upcoming week. Parking spaces close to the store were taken, so Grace let me out a block from the entrance and said to go ahead. She'd park wherever she could and come inside to stay cool. She didn't need groceries.

I was sweating by the time I entered Whole Foods. It smelled good and felt cool, but I didn't intend to dally. I went straight to the

peanut butter, grape jelly and bread sections, then to dairy for milk.
I considered buying loose organic vegetables. When I headed for
the veggies, I saw Penelope Farquhar mooning over produce.
I slipped up fairly close with only a single bin separating us.
She didn't recognize me under Charlie's hat. I wanted to surprise
her to see her reaction. Directly in her line of vision, I swished off
the hat and glasses.

"Oh! It's you. I didn't expect..."

"To see me out of jail?"

"Well, I heard..."

"You heard right. They let me out temporarily. I'm a
weekender. Have to report back." I figured she wouldn't know the
difference.

"A weekender? For..."

"Breaking into the science lab. Not for killing Eric Lager."

"Lager. They know he was murdered."

Penelope had just uttered a declarative sentence. How did she
know he'd been murdered?

"Yes. It was pretty obvious somebody had killed him. They're
working on who and how. They found the bottle of nasal spray near
his body. That ought to help."

"Nasal spray?"

"That's right. Probably has a ton of fingerprints on it." I waited
a few beats for that to soak in. "I need to get some veggies before I
go back." I grabbed carrots, broccoli and cauliflower. "I'll get salt
and pepper shakers so I can nibble these en route back to the
detention center."

She stared at me like she was in shock. I was glad she was too
stunned to wonder how a jailbird could wander freely about.

"I better get some fruit." I headed for the next bin. "They don't
give you much in jail."

"Fruit," she muttered, as I sashayed past her to checkout.

The lines were long. Before I got there, I saw Grace sitting in a
chair near the exit. She pointed to herself, made car-driving
motions and left.

I found the express line, paid and skedaddled out the door. Despite replacing the glasses and hat, I still squinted into the sun. I saw Grace's red Honda at the corner and took long strides to overtake her. She was blocking another car and was about to pull away when I leaped into the passenger seat.

"Home, James."

"That was pretty quick."

"Yep. And Penelope Farquhar was there. She was amazed to see me. She knew Lager was murdered. She thought I'd been arrested for killing him and was still in jail. After she thinks about what I said, I bet it'll scare the greens out of her."

The light turned, and Grace squealed onto Basse Road.

Fifty-Two

When we arrived at Grace's house, I asked her to incarcerate Boffo in the bathroom. I didn't want him barking at me while I trekked across our yards toward home.

I peered out her back window to make sure nobody was casing her house or mine, then slipped across the grass and into the back door of my house. My belongings were strewn about in the same deplorable condition I'd left them.

I plodded to the kitchen, threw out the wilted inhabitants of my refrigerator and refilled the crispers with fresh greens. If I made many more trips to Whole Foods, I might grow to detest produce.

In my bathroom I got a good look at myself in Charlie's fishing hat. No wonder I'd startled Penelope. I'd reorganize the bathroom and kitchen later.

When Sam called, I had to repeat plausible reasons why I should return to class the next morning. I also needed to rehearse what I planned to say to class members and think about how to protect myself if I got into trouble before SAPD could reach me.

In the living room, I pulled down my window shades and admired my antique secretary desk captured at auction. I concluded I had to reorder my living area and bedroom. Returning belongings to their proper place, I mused about how strange we are; we miss only what we're in imminent danger of losing.

It occurred to me that if my scheme to go back on campus to oust the killer failed, I'd disappoint a lot of "Dear Aggie" readers. I grabbed the stack of mail I'd tossed on the coffee table while straightening up, flipped through and opened a letter.

Dear Aggie,

I've taken your advice. I've decided that fifty-three isn't old, just a midway blip. I've registered at college for Art History and am taking watercolor classes. My husband is scared I'll change and he won't know me. My kids grumble that when they need me, I'm not always around. Am I making a mistake?

Purposeful but panicky,
Pamela

Dear Purposeful Pamela,

Don't panic. You're not making a mistake. You're figuring out who you are after caring for others for umpteen years. Pursue your interests and talents. How often did you make it possible for your loved ones to pursue theirs? If you think you can do it, then you can. Let your family know that the happier, more fulfilled you is still there. They'll get it. Stay on the Yellow Brick Road. There's more joy ahead.

Energized and eager,
Aggie

Having reminded Pamela and myself to take charge of our destinies, I was ready to get back to business. I plopped in the chair, pulled down the lid to my secretary desk to expose my computer and directed WebCrawler to search information about wearing a wire. The process looked uncomfortable. It appeared the device could easily be detected—not, it seemed to me, a good

190 Nancy G. West

solution for a person accosted by a killer. Sidetracked to other
devices in the spy field, I'd started yawning when Meredith called.
"Shall I pick you up for class tomorrow? I'll feel safer if we go
together."

What a dear friend. I didn't want to endanger her. "No, thanks.
I have a couple of errands to run beforehand. I'll alert Sam. He
won't let me out of SAPD's sight."

"All right, if you're sure. I'll see you in class. Be careful."

I'd barely replaced the receiver when Sam called.

"Are you locked in? No problems?"

"I'm locked in, the alarm is set and I'm fine. Did SAPD learn
anything new about Eric Lager's murder?"

"Not yet. They expect to have autopsy and toxicology reports
tomorrow. I'll let you know. Are you still determined to attend
class?"

"I think it's perfectly safe. How could anybody bother me in
broad daylight? I don't think I can wear a wire, Sam. If somebody
grabs me, they're bound to discover it."

"It does take practice to wear one inconspicuously. I'll have
somebody follow you to campus."

"All right. I have to leave early. I need to buy toiletries at
HEB."

"What time?"

"About nine a.m. That should give me plenty of time to stop at
the store and get a good parking space on campus before my ten-
thirty class."

"I'll tell Officer Mulhaney to be at your house. He'll be in a
dark blue unmarked Dodge Charger."

"Don't worry. I'll be fine. Sleep tight."

"You too. Be very careful tomorrow, Aggie."

I had a new idea and dialed Meredith.

Fifty-Three

Although my house was secure, Sam's warnings had made me uneasy. After I put on my Garfield sleep shirt and brushed my teeth, I repeated N-E-E-T-T several times, accompanying each letter with an attack on the vulnerable parts of my assailant's head. I practiced until I felt comfortable with my ability to execute the moves.

Satisfied, I laid out clothes for the next day: cool khaki slacks and a loose, billowy blouse. Both had pockets for pens, pencils and miscellaneous items. I'd carry a small purse and a binder for taking notes.

I flopped into bed, turned out the lights and pictured the people in tomorrow's class. Odds were the killer would be there. If the killer was one of the scientists I met at the memorial service, I hoped my announcement in class would be startling enough to spread to them like wildfire.

My plan was to make the killer think I'd found evidence in the lab which would incriminate the culprit.

I mentally rehearsed what I'd say.

I knew one thing: whatever words I chose, the looks on my classmates' faces would be priceless.

I set my morning alarm for thirty minutes earlier than usual so I could spend fifteen minutes hugging my pillow and gazing at my beautifully organized bedroom. After I got up to brush my teeth, I pantomimed N-E-E-T-T moves until I was starving. I downed two eggs and toast for protein and carbs.

It was almost nine. Dressed in my monochrome clothes, I peered through a slit by the front window shade. The plainclothes cop slumped in his car with the bill of his hat pulled down and watched my bungalow.

Unlocking the kitchen door to the garage, I grabbed a length of heavy-duty twine hanging on the garage wall in case I needed to tie somebody up, pushed it into a pants pocket under my long blouse and slid into Albatross. SAPD's search police had tossed papers from Albatross's glove compartment and side pockets onto the front seat and floor, but it didn't really matter. They wouldn't have found anything interesting. I flung my binder and purse, with Charlie's fishing hat stuffed inside, on top of the litter and pushed the button to raise the garage door. The creaking door was sure to get the officer's attention. I backed out, squelched the urge to wave at Officer Mulhaney and drove to the Basse Road HEB. I parked at the east end of the store where Mulhaney couldn't miss spotting Albatross.

I walked in, headed straight for the pharmacy and found a nasal spray bottle. The brand was common, and the plastic bottle was identical to the one Carmody used and the one lying by Eric. I thought it might come in handy. I looked around for pepper spray. They apparently didn't stock it.

A floppy-brimmed sun hat on sale near the register caught my eye. I grabbed it, paid, walked to the exit farthest from where I entered and peeked out. To the right, I could see the tail end of Meredith's car around the corner of the store. She had the engine running.

Mulhaney slouched in his car past the other end of HEB. I pressed the hat down on my head, slipped out the door, dashed to the corner and jumped into Meredith's Taurus.

"Don't squeal the tires. I don't want to attract attention. Whip around these businesses, get back on Basse, cut through streets and wind your way back to Broadway."

"I'm not sure why we're doing this," she said. "Sam will have police at the university anyway. Ditching this officer will just tick him off. He's right. You are stubborn."

"I hate to be told what I can and cannot do and be followed like a common criminal. Thanks for picking me up. Drive to Best Buy between Isom and San Pedro, okay?"

"Why are we going there?"

"I need to pick up a couple of good pens. It'll be open."

She sighed. "Whatever. Just don't break any laws."

I gave her a sullen look, but I really couldn't blame her.

Fifty-Four

When we arrived at the school, lots near the main building were full, so we had to park in the back lot and walk. It was just as well. I told Meredith to go ahead. If Sam or another policeman saw her, I asked her to say we brought separate cars. I didn't want her to get in trouble. I just wanted to be left alone on the way to class. I had a lot on my mind. Donning sunglasses and Charlie's fishing hat, I took a circuitous route to the main building.

Before I went inside, I took off the hat and walked around slowly before I entered. Any policeman who saw me could report to Sam that I was safe, well, and practically sitting in class.

When I entered the room, every pair of eyes flipped toward me. I scanned the inhabitants. Penelope Farquhar stared at me with a mixture of apprehension and disbelief, her face contorted like a mutated mushroom. Meredith came in and took a seat. Everybody in the room looked familiar, including the postdoc scientists sitting on either side of Brandy Crystal.

My eyes rested on her attire. The orange neon Lycra shirt pasting her body would stop a driver faster than a street sign. Thick mascara on her lashes accentuated her black spiked hair. The image of a porcupine skittered across my mind. A shiny black miniskirt barely covered the tops of her lanky bronze legs. Tanned or not, my legs would never look like that. She'd given up grunge-style socks for flip-flops and orange neon toenails.

One of the postdocs kept touching her arm. I thought the man she'd kissed under the tree had been taller. She looked in my direction, ignoring the man touching her and the younger man with the large nose watching her chest rise and fall underneath the Lycra.

When Dr. Hortense Bigsby entered the room, she looked my way and did a double take. Then she cleared her throat, stiffened her neck, adjusted her spectacles and straightened to full department-chair height. She was determined to maintain her dignity, appear professional and lead class.

"I'm sure you all know," she began, "about Dr. Lager's tragic death. He is a great loss to our city and a profound loss to our university and the scientific community. He will be honored at a service here at Memorial Chapel tomorrow at one p.m. The most we can do for him now is to honor him by discussing the subject he loved most, human genetics."

She paused for a few beats. Before anyone could formulate questions about Eric Lager, she proceeded to lecture on subjects we'd already covered. She seemed determined to run out the clock without touching the issue of why a second professor had died. She finally ran out of things to say and asked if anybody had questions. Students swiveled in their chairs, their eyes eventually snapping toward me.

I stood. "I don't have a question, Dr. Bigsby, but I'm sure you've all heard I was the one who found Dr. Lager's body in the science lab." You could have heard a molecule drop. "I was indeed in the lab—when I shouldn't have been—hoping to find reasons for Dr. Carmody's sudden death. Did he encounter something toxic in the lab? Was there some hint to indicate why Dr. Carmody had been ill? How could such a famous, healthy person just drop dead?"

That was mostly poppycock, but I was really getting into it. Everybody looked stunned, like they were watching the horror movie *Scream 2*.

I lowered my voice almost to a whisper. "I looked around the lab for quite a while. I didn't find as much as I'd hoped to." I paused to let the implication of that line sink in. They leaned forward.

"It was dark," I continued, "and my flashlight wasn't working too well. Unfortunately, I was concentrating on my task when I stumbled into...well, you know...Professor Lager." I bowed my head. There were intakes of breath. I let appropriate time pass before I raised my head, eyes moist.

"The campus police saw the glow from my flashlight and burst in. Unfortunately, they entered at the moment I found..." I started coughing. "I'm sorry. It's just too hard for me to go on."

After an uncomfortable silence, a student spoke. "We heard they took you to jail."

It wasn't hard for me to conjure up tears thinking about that. I sputtered and wiped my eyes and nose while they waited.

"What did you find?" one student asked. "In the lab?" She held her breath.

I started sniffling again. "I'm sorry," I peeped in a quiet voice. "It's very difficult for me to discuss it."

"Do the police think you killed him?" Brandy blurted. "Are you going back to jail?"

I let the lingering silence float around the room. People muttered in low tones, compelled to make conjectures before I could even respond.

When it was nearly time for class to be over, I lifted my chin, closed my eyes and shook my head in pious denial. "The police have evidence that I didn't do it. That's why they let me out of jail."

Class ended. A few students came up to express their support that I'd been sprung and hadn't killed anybody. Nobody mentioned Dr. Carmody. Several students looked at me askance, not sure what to believe. They milled around, making private comments to each another. They finally meandered toward the door, not knowing how to solicit more information about who or what killed the two men.

As the first group reached the threshold, Professor Bigsby raised her arms like Moses parting the sea. She smiled warmly.

"I hate to leave you all in such turmoil near the beginning of a semester." Students gaped. "The deaths of these men were tragic, and we will continue to grieve their loss. But, as promising students of science, you need to know that they left us a legacy."

People raised their eyebrows.

"They made a breakthrough—albeit a small one—before they left this earth."

"Wow."

"Awesome."

"How wonderful!"

"Ms. Mundeen may have seen hints of it in the lab." She peered at me over her spectacles. "But," she clasped her hands in regret, "the university president and board won't let me share it with you so soon after Dr. Lager's death. After we honor him tomorrow, perhaps toward the end of this week or next, I will be able to share the news."

Everyone clapped. Hungry for good news, they nodded and smiled at Dr. Bigsby as we streamed into the hall.

Fifty-Five

I pointed to Brandy and her entourage and whispered to Meredith, "Let's have lunch with them and see what we can learn."

She rolled her eyes but plodded alongside me to the cafeteria. I made sure we kept up the pace so we'd be right behind them. I saw a couple of guys in plainclothes who might be cops and ignored them. But one came over and pulled me aside. I asked Meredith to go ahead and stick with the threesome.

The plainclothes cop got in my face. "You're Aggie, right? Sam said to tell you he's not happy you ditched his patrolman."

"I'm just going to lunch, okay? With a hundred other people. I'm starving. Tell him I'll be home in about an hour."

"Be careful what you eat. And don't go wandering around campus."

Cops were paranoid. "I'll eat something bottled or from a sealed container. I just want to be a regular student back at school, as though everything was normal." I whirled and ran to catch up with Meredith.

We entered the cafeteria and got in line behind Brandy and her fan club. Whenever one of them looked my way between choosing their cafeteria items, I smiled sweetly.

After they paid, Brandy purposefully chose a small table, but I motioned to Meredith, and we pulled chairs up to the corners.

"I hate being crowded when I eat," Brandy pouted.

"Me too," I said. "We wanted to visit with our classmates." The men ogled Meredith, happy to follow my suggestion.

"I'm Aggie Mundeen," I said to the younger man who'd previously had his eyes glued to Brandy's orange Lycra. "We never formally introduced ourselves at Dr. Carmody's memorial."

He managed to tear his eyes away from Meredith. "Phillip Delay. I'm a postdoc in the Lawson lab."

"This is my friend, Meredith Laughlin."

He scanned her again, waist to face. "Pleased to meet you."

"And what is your field?" I asked, trying to regain his attention.

"Biogenetics."

"Ah. Then you've been following the work of Professors Carmody and Lager?"

"Yes. I've visited with them several times at conferences. Stanley," he indicated his friend, "invited me to stay with him so we could see their setup and attend a few classes. And now to lose them both. Such a tragedy." He stabbed a French fry.

"I imagine you got to know the professors quite well and observed their lab operations."

"Yes."

I looked at Stanley. "And you're a professor here?"

"A visiting professor in the biology department this semester while Dr. Smith takes her sabbatical. Stanley Bly." He nodded at Meredith. She acknowledged him and took another bite of her sandwich.

"I hope to spend more time here," Delay said. He slid his hand over Brandy's arm. She glanced at him and batted her lashes. Then she glared at me like she'd like to poison my food.

I scanned their faces. "What did you think of Dr. Bigsby's forthcoming announcement?"

"Fascinating," Bly mouthed through his French fries. "Carmody and Lager indicated they had something coming up that might interest us."

"Do you know what it was?"

"Well, no," Bly said. "We have ideas, of course..."

"Of course. You must stay for the revelation then," I said.

Delay slid his leg against Brandy and reached under the table. She didn't seem to mind. "For the revelation," he said. "Yes. I must stay."

I thought Brandy had probably revealed everything. Perhaps even her lethal relationship with two dead men.

We had almost finished eating, and I didn't want to spend too long on campus. Sam might have me nabbed and hauled to his office. We said our goodbyes and carried trays to the trash bin. I caught our lunch mates following us with their eyes. The men eyeballed Meredith. Brandy looked disgustedly at me.

"Meredith, I need to use the facilities before we leave."

"Okay. I'll get the car and bring it around front. It's so darn hot, I'll take my time walking over there. Then I'll take you to retrieve Albatross."

"Great." I debated with myself on a quick trip to the bathroom. Bigsby's announcement didn't sound quite right. Yet she was the most apt to know if the professors had made a discovery. She and Brandy.

Bly and Delay didn't seem surprised by Bigsby's announcement. Had Brandy already told them? Had the three of them colluded to kill Carmody and Lager for their discovery? Whatever Bigsby planned to reveal might be key to who murdered both scientists. Some evidence of the breakthrough had to be in the lab. And the key to exonerating me as a suspect. I had a hearing to face and no evidence to prove that I didn't kill Eric Lager. My feet started itching.

Fifty-Six

I left the cafeteria when bunches of students were leaving. Slipping into the middle of a group, I kept pace, scouting for plainclothes cops. I saw two of them, but they were apparently looking for a single person or two people walking together. Staying with the group until it began to break up, I joined another cluster of people heading in the general direction of the science building.

In order for classes to continue without interruption, Meredith said the police had agreed not to post crime scene tape at the site. I hoped they'd left the building open for daytime use without stationing officers at the front and back. I also hoped SAPD officers were nearby, scouting the area.

I glanced up at the clock tower. It was twelve forty-five p.m. I would wander into the lab, casually stroll around to see if anything new caught my eye and leave. I wouldn't touch anything or inhale anything, and I'd be gone in ten minutes.

Blending with a group who apparently had afternoon classes in the science building, I melded with them as they entered the front door. There were no officers in sight. I slowed my pace. Once the students moved toward their classrooms, I dashed into the lab. It was quiet. Nobody was there. Perfect.

Clutching my binder, I patted my blouse pocket for pens and fingered the lump underneath my waistband. I had put the nasal spray in my pants pockets.

I scooted through the lab into the small room to check the back door. I wanted it left open in case I needed to make a hasty exit.

Shades were drawn on the lab's bank of windows to keep out the heat. It was a bit dim in the lab without lighting. I was getting my bearings in the main room, looking around at the cabinets, adjusting my eyes to subdued light, when a figure appeared in the doorway from the storage room. It was Brandy! She'd changed her clothes. She wore the slinky green shorts and stretched pink camisole she'd worn at her apartment. Had she come to rendezvous with somebody in the lab?

I blinked. Brandy seemed taller than I remembered. She'd put on fishnet stockings and ballet shoes that made her legs seem even longer. When she strolled toward me, boobs leading, I recognized the long stride of Olive Oyl.

I squinted. "Dr. Bigsby, is that you?" With dark hair spiked to perfection, eyes lined in musky brown, and lashes heavy with mascara, she looked enough like Brandy to fool anyone.

She twisted her lipsticked mouth into a seductive sneer. "It's not hard to be a slut if you work at it."

"I guess not. But why? Why are you here? Dressed like that?" Had she snapped from perpetually watching Brandy flirt with all the men? I could appreciate that sentiment.

"You've been here a few times before, Agatha. I think it's time we have a chat. Just a minute." She disappeared into the small back room, and I heard the door lock click.

Before I could think what to do, she reappeared. She strode to the front door of the lab, locked it and yanked down the shade.

"The students don't need to use the lab today."

She turned and walked toward me. As she came closer, I couldn't help but focus on her camisole. Something was in there. Something had been added to the flat surface I'd seen wrinkle when I visited her office. Falsies. With push-ups underneath. Which meant the camisole was holding it all together.

She gave me a disgusted look. "You were in here visiting with Eric Lager, weren't you? Before somebody killed him."

"Yes. He took me on a tour of the lab."

"He could be a nice man. Sometimes. I'll bet he offered you V8 juice." She dipped false lashes over half-closed lids.

"Why, yes, come to think of it. It was a hot day. The drink was refreshing. Why?"

"He wanted your DNA, sweetie. He added a little Taq polymerase to make millions of copies of some of your genes." She hoisted her chin in snobbish annoyance. "How we scientists have the patience to deal with ignoramuses like you, I'll never know. He separated out genes from your DNA and mixed different substances with your gene specimens to watch the effect."

She smirked. "Science always comes first, you know. I thought it was a lovely idea. Come here." She beckoned with a skinny, crooked finger. "I'll show you."

I didn't like the direction this was taking. But I might be about to learn about Carmody and Lager's anti-aging discovery. I followed her to the incubator with my feet itching. She opened the door and peered in at an array of agar plates, each one hosting cells with my genes quivering in various substances.

She was a big woman. Bent over, she reminded me of the song, "The bear went over the mountain..." I checked the back of her hair. Where was her bun? From the lump at her crown, I surmised she'd tucked it under the spiky black wig. The mound gave her head an egg shape. And a sturdy docking station where she could anchor the wig.

She moved to the side to make sure I appreciated the importance of what I was viewing.

"See there?" She wiggled her pointy digit. "They're all yours—each a little clump of your very own genes, each group thriving in a different medium." She gleefully tented her fingers together. "With goodies added. Changing your genes into God knows what." She looked smug.

"Take that plate, for instance." She pointed. "The genes in those cells were drenched with telomerase. See how they proliferated? So many squiggly little darlings. The overabundance of telomerase made them multiply *way* too fast. They turned into busy little cancer cells." She paused to let the horror of the diabolical experiment sink in. "With a good dose of those, you wouldn't have to worry anymore about aging." She threw her head back and chortled. Her wig bounced.

"See the next plate over? There's less telomerase on those cells...maybe just enough to lengthen telomeres at the end of your chromosomes. Help them proliferate properly. Maintain their immune properties. Wouldn't that be nice?" She chuckled and batted lashes that looked like they'd been stuck on with Gorilla Glue. "You'd much rather have those genes back in your body, now wouldn't you?"

A chill slid down my back. I started wondering if I could outrun her fishnet legs and get out of there.

"Now those," she pointed to a plate whose contents looked almost dried up, "those were mixed with progerin. It'll take a few more days for them to die." She crossed her arms. I shuddered, remembering children with progeria aging rapidly and dying prematurely.

"You might find those other specimens particularly interesting." Her index finger pointed across a series of plates placed side by side in a row. "Eric extracted your APOE genes and cultured copies so he could mix each one with a different enzyme. Hmm. All those mixtures look pretty active. Which combination do you think will produce Alzheimer's first? Maybe some protein will stop the APOE genes from mutating at all, so you'll never get Alzheimer's. Who knows? Sort of like Russian roulette, isn't it?" She threw her head back and emitted an insane cackle.

"I'd better go."

"Oh, no. We're not nearly finished. You want to know about their latest discoveries, don't you?" She grabbed my arm. Her hand, lengthened with false pointed nails, squeezed my arm with the strength of raptors' talons. "This next set of experiments is the most interesting."

Still gripping my arm, she pointed to a set of agar plates occupying an entire shelf. "You remember the daf-2 gene? The one that affects the expression of other genes that speed up or slow 'downstream' genes believed to be earmarks for aging? I know you're particularly interested in stopping the aging process." She paused and waited for me to nod.

"Kermit Carmody was especially interested in the daf-2 gene." She looked smug. "But it was Eric who managed to get your DNA so they could experiment with your genes."

I was trying to remain rational and keep our conversation on a scientific plane. I thought she had killed both men and lured me to the lab. I had to figure out a way to make her confess and then escape.

"Dr. Carmody and Eric worked well together?"

"For a while." She threw her head back, squawked a laugh, then shook herself back to seriousness. Her wig settled.

Once they'd made their discovery, Eric invited me to the lab to scare me so I wouldn't come back to pry. He must have hit me on the head for good measure.

Bigsby rearranged the mounds on her chest and pointed back to the last set of plates.

"Kermit figured out how to isolate the downstream genes," she said, "but Eric wanted to test them using live, active specimens from a subject approaching middle age. Fortunately, you were amusingly available and big on V8 juice."

It was one thing to contribute to science, but my fear of Hortense Bigsby was growing by the second. She got behind me, nudged me up to the incubator so I couldn't break away and pointed at the first plate in the set.

"That daf-2 gene? The one right there? It has a daf-16 gene in its pathway. We insert something into daf-2 and then see what daf-16 does. Neat, huh?"

She was breathing in my ear. Her proximity creeped me out. How could I get away from this madwoman?

"We see what various enzymes added to daf-2 will do to daf-16. Then we pick the enzymes that seem to affect daf-16 the most, and we add another downstream gene to the plate. It's so exciting! A chain reaction of mutating genes. It's like watching a new civilization breed." With that, she clamped me in a bear hug from the rear. The bottle of nasal spray popped out of my pants pocket and hit the floor.

"Where'd you get that?" she screamed, crushing me tighter.

I bit her arm, jerked my elbows up to break her hold and stomped her mammoth foot hard as I could. When she stumbled backward, her wig came loose. It was still moored, but now it was flapping around the back of her head. Wild-eyed, she rushed me.

Fifty-Seven

I charged for the door. She leaped behind me and grabbed me around the neck in a headlock. I bit her arm. She shrieked but was still able to tug me toward the electrophoresis machine and power box. With her arm mashing my windpipe, I couldn't scream. I tried to maneuver my leg behind one of her legs to throw her off balance. But with her dragging me, I couldn't do it.

She tightened her hold around my neck, reached for the cable and plugged the power box into the DNA-separating machine. She looked down with scorn, her mouth contorting into a reptilian sneer.

"Why don't we stick your hands in some gel and into the chamber to see what three hundred volts does? Burn off your skin? Shock the bejeebers out of you?"

"It'll shock you too," I croaked. "We're connected."

When she relaxed her hold, I bit her arm again.

"Aagh!"

She was too tall for me to poke her eyes or smack her eardrums. I started to run. I was halfway to the door when she tackled me and knocked me to the floor. Stunned and breathless, I felt her plop down and pin me by sitting on my backside.

"That's enough, bitch. You're all alike. You. Penelope. Brandy. The lot of you. All flirty and cute and curious. And ignorant!"

I heard her open a drawer and grab something. Perched on my rear end, she leaned forward and dangled rubber tubing in front of my face.

"Let's tie you up and see what kind of experiments we can do."

I squirmed, but she was too strong. She yanked my wrists together behind my back and tied them with tubing. Since I might be about to die, I decided to try and get on Hortense's wavelength.

"Brandy really flirted with Dr. Carmody, didn't she?"

She pulled the tubing tighter. "We were lovers, Kermit and I, until Sleazy Pants showed up and started twitting around the Boston lab." Hortense was so upset, she had trouble tying the knot around my hands.

The image of Kermit and Olive Oyl making love triggered my cough reflex, but with my breathing capacity compromised, I only sputtered.

"I took it as long as I could, watching her sashay in and out, flipping her boobs around. She could *never* help Kermit in his work like I could."

I squeezed out a comment that I knew would get a rise. "Perhaps Brandy had other attributes."

To my amazement, Hortense started sniffling. When I heard her snatch a Kleenex from a box on a nearby desk, I twisted my wrists to loosen the tubing. When she raised a hand to wipe her face and honked into the Kleenex, I pulled against the binding.

"I couldn't stand it anymore," she sniffed, "so I accepted this position at UHT. Darned if the university didn't pay him big bucks so he'd come here." She honked again. "And Sleazy Pants came with him."

I spewed words out in puffs. "And they were...getting close...to determining...the sequence...of anti-aging genes."

"Yes. And how to affect their activity. Kermit and I could have discovered the secrets of anti-aging. Working together, we could have been famous! He could never have left me then."

"But they were getting so close," I said, "he and Eric and Brandy. You decided you had to do something."

She sniffed back a glob of tears. "I couldn't let them find the secrets to aging. That would cement Kermit's relationship with *her*. He would live longer, and she would have him forever."

That didn't sound like such a great deal to me.

"That could not happen!" she shouted.

"So you killed him."

"I only meant to weaken his immune system so he'd stay out of the lab long enough for me to get rid of Brandy," she wailed. "But the fungus overwhelmed him."

She sat back on her haunches, sobbing and grabbed the Kleenex box. I could breathe better, but my legs were still pinned. I had to make her confess that she killed Eric.

I heard her sigh. I thought she was so busy nursing her grief she'd lost interest in me. She might have, if I hadn't piped up. I couldn't resist needling her.

"Then Brandy started helping Eric, scientifically and in other ways. And he began to realize what you'd done to Carmody."

I heard a growl in her throat. "Brandy helped him, all right. That's when I decided she'd done all the damage she was going to do. Anybody can dress like this and seduce men. Don't you see? It's so meaningless. Yet men keep falling for it. Dr. Carmody admired the complete opposite type of woman, a serious, brilliant scientist like me. Until Brandy took him down."

Hortense Bigsby had tried to perfect herself into what she thought Carmody wanted. When that didn't work, she flipped and became Brandy.

"You knew you could be like Brandy. Better than Brandy, if you wanted to."

"Exactly."

I sensed that Hortense was leaning back—probably admiring her boobs.

"And you understood what they were accomplishing in the lab. You could continue the experiments without any of them. With Carmody and Eric both gone, Brandy had no reason to hang around. She couldn't pull off a scientific breakthrough without them. She might book the next flight back to Boston."

"Precisely. But Eric had to be eliminated."

"Now that you've killed him, you're free to carry on. I could help you," I said. "I've studied enough to know what you're trying to do. I could help carry out experiments under your direction. My name wouldn't be associated with the research, of course. I don't have the qualifications. But you would be famous. I could use my column to help make you famous."

Her voice grated like gravel. "But you would know I killed Kermit and Eric. That bit of information would make it difficult for us to work together."

She got off my legs and yanked me to my feet. My knees wobbled.

"Let's see what kind of lab accident we can have," she said.

With my hands still bound at my back, she headlocked me again and dragged me toward the incubator. I hadn't noticed the small box on the adjoining countertop labeled "ethidium bromide." She opened it, grabbed a spoon from a drawer, scooped out a purplish-red mound of powder and held it under my nose.

I turned my head away so I wouldn't inhale it, but she had a boa-constrictor hold around my neck. I finally had to breathe, and I inhaled the deadly stuff. I twisted my head to make sure I sneezed as much of it as I could back in her face. We would die together.

With both of us sneezing violently, I slipped out of her headlock, wrangled one of my hands out of the binding and yanked at her camisole. A falsie popped out followed by a wire-supported rubber crescent. There was nothing left but flat fabric with a small wrinkle.

"That did it!" The hatred in her eyes could have shattered a test tube. She grabbed my arm and almost jerked it out of the socket, yanking my wrist back to retie me. She saw the bulge in my pants pocket and yanked out my heavy-duty twine. "How convenient," she sneered.

I'd planned to use it to tie up the killer, but she wrapped it around me and tied me to the heavy metal pull on a locked cabinet. It was probably the cabinet where Dr. Carmody kept his research notes and list of trusted scientists. Sam could retrieve them after they removed my body.

She rummaged through other drawers and came back with a syringe. Holding it in front of my nose, she slowly pushed in the plunger. "Let's see which of your mutated genes your body likes the best."

Cackling insanely, she strutted to the incubator, swinging the syringe back and forth, and opened the door.

"This APOE gene looks good. But not everybody's APOE gene morphs into Alzheimer's disease. It doesn't happen all that often. Not a sure thing. Too bad. We'll skip that one for now."

Why hadn't we died from inhaling ethidium bromide? It should have been quicker.

She pointed the syringe at the plates lined up on a shelf. "There's those little daf-2 darlings with their downstream genes." She shook her head. "It's not a slam dunk how one will change the next one, though—especially if some disgustingly healthy lifestyle habit of yours changes how they act once they're back in your body." I felt nauseous.

She put a hand on her bony hip. "Okay, so what else? The progerin looks good. Everybody is born with some in their body." She wrinkled her face. "We're not sure how much more it takes to set you on the path to destruction..." I hoped for a quick death.

"I've got it." Her wig flopped around. "We'll use your genes that are *drenched* with telomerase. Those little boogers are proliferating like crazy. They're not going to stop when I inject them into you. I wonder what organs they'll go for first. Your liver? Maybe a bone? Your heart? Your brain? You'll always wonder, won't you, where they'll attack first. While you worry about it, you can look forward to a slow, agonizing death."

I was about to black out. Either the bromide was working, or she was scaring me to death. I watched her remove a plate and suck its revolting mixture into the syringe. I had to think of something fast before I started hyperventilating. She slithered toward me with an eel-like stride. Like slow motion in a dream, she unveiled her teeth in a wicked smile. The room was fading.

Her talons sank into my arm and brought me back.

"I'll have to loosen the rope to get one of your arms—bring it around so I can inject this directly into a vein. Works faster."

She had to get really close to reach around me. When I felt the rope loosen, she was right up against me. With the top of my head, I headbutted her under the chin as hard as I could. She staggered. I had to use my defense training before she fell back too far. I step-kicked. With the bottom of my foot, I caught her full force right in the kneecap. She screamed with pain, fell back, clipped her head on a counter and fell to the floor, unconscious.

She looked pretty disheveled. One boob pointed skyward. On the other side, her chest was flat. Her black wig flew to the back of her head, barely attached to her bun. When she came to, she'd be in a lot of pain. But she wouldn't be able to get up. Igor had made that clear. I'd torn up everything around her knee that held her leg bones together.

I brought my hand around, ripped off the rubber tubing and started wiggling my body out of the twine. The police were so slow, I'd probably be free before they got there.

I felt for the lump under my waistband, pushed the "on" button and stuck my fingers in my ears. It was amazing how loud a personal alarm could sound powered with nothing but batteries.

Fifty-Eight

Sam burst through the lab door followed by two other cops in civvies, guns drawn.

He was wild-eyed. "I can't believe you're in here!" he shouted. "Are you all right? What's that screeching noise? Who's that on the floor?" He leaned toward her. "What happened to her?"

I pushed the "off" button on my personal alarm. "She has torn ligaments and cartilage that held her upper and lower leg bones together. And a torn meniscus—the padding between the bones. You better call an ambulance. She can't get up."

He pointed to one of the cops. "Call EMS." He walked closer to her and squinted down. "Who is she?"

"Dr. Hortense Bigsby. Head of the biology department. Former lover of Dr. Kermit Carmody. Revolting thought, isn't it?"

"I'd never have recognized her." He furrowed his brow. "What did you do to her?"

"She came in here dressed like Brandy Crystal, Eric Lager's lab assistant and Dr. Bigsby's competition for Dr. Carmody. She attacked me. I rearranged her attire."

"You certainly did. I doubt they can put her back together."

I grinned.

"What was that screeching siren?"

"My personal alarm." I held up the battery-operated alarm on the keychain I'd stuffed under my waistband. "Best Buy. Twelve dollars."

"You're kidding."

"Nope. And I learned self-defense. That's how I fought her off."

"You knew she'd be here? And you came here, despite what I told you?" His eyes were bulging. He looked like an owl.

"She announced in class that Carmody and Lager had made a breakthrough against aging before they died."

"And you just had to come see what that was." He shook his head. "Did you find anything?"

I decided not to mention she'd lured me to the lab to kill me.

"I found a bunch of weird concoctions she said were mixed with my genes. They're over there in that incubator. She tried to inject me with them."

He paled. "But she didn't do it."

"No."

He turned to one of the officers. "Grady, get the lab guys over here. And a chemist. And a geneticist. And whatever other kind of scientist they think they might need. I want everybody wearing protective gear."

"There might be ethidium bromide over there on that counter. The purplish-red powder. It's a carcinogen. If you inhale enough, it can kill you."

"Did you inhale it? Is that what's on your face?"

"She shook it under my nose. We both inhaled it."

"Okay. I'm calling Hazmat. Everybody out in the hall. You too, Aggie. You guys stay in the hall, pull up that door shade and watch through the glass. Don't let EMS in until Hazmat clears it. I'll handcuff Bigsby in case she wakes up."

He pulled on disposable gloves and yanked a mask from his pocket. "Put this on, Aggie. I carry it from past experience with spitters. Go sit in the hall. Do. Not. Move. You guys have masks?" he asked the officers. "If not, tie handkerchiefs over your nose and mouth."

I backed into the hall, watching Sam hold his breath while he tied a handkerchief over his nose and mouth and handcuffed Dr. Bigsby. I was glad he was experienced enough to carry a mask, but I wished he'd brought more than one. He joined us in the hall.

"Where's Meredith?" I asked.

"She called us in a panic and said she was afraid you might come here. I told her to go to HEB in case you showed up at your car." He punched numbers into his phone, called the officer nearest the store and told him to find Meredith and tell her he'd found me.

"She'll be pretty angry."

"I'm not too happy with you myself."

"Hortense Bigsby killed Carmody and Eric Lager," I said through the mask.

"How do you know?"

I pulled the pen from my pocket and handed it to him. "It's a recorder pen. Voice-activated. It was expensive, but everything is on there. Even why she did it. Can you drive me to my car at HEB? And have the officer tell Meredith again that we're fine? And that I'll call her later?"

He squinted his eyes closed. He might have been counting to ten.

Fifty-Nine

I heard sirens and tiptoed so I could see out the front of the science building. Two red fire trucks and two white EMS units with red and blue decals screeched to a stop, sirens blaring. Students approached the perimeter of the vehicles. A fire department officer had to shoo them off the grass.

Sam and I walked out onto the steps.

Two firemen jumped from the first truck, dressed in space suits and hoods, and came blasting toward us. "Hazmat Entry Team, San Antonio Fire Department."

A voice called through a megaphone near a fire truck. "District Chief Lansing here. You the officer who called?"

Sam nodded and shouted back, "Detective Sam Vanderhoven, SAPD."

Lansing said, "I'm directing the Hazmat Unit. Where's the hot zone?"

Sam pointed. "Inside the building. Lab to the right. We have one victim here and one inside."

Two Hazmat team members charged into the building and two more loped toward us. "Sit down, miss. We have to see if you're contaminated. You too, officers." They put equipment on the steps and started testing the four of us.

"You were in there, miss?" he asked me, breathing from inside his bubble.

"Yes, sir," I burbled through my mask. "Aggie Mundeen."

"She inhaled ethidium bromide powder in that science lab,"

Sam said. "We're from SAPD and just got here." He pointed to his fellow officers. "Officers Martinez and Grady."

The fireman pulled my mask down and swabbed my face. "Is this the bromide?"

I nodded. He removed all he could and put it in a container to test it. Sam and I held our breath.

The fireman sat back on his haunches. "It's talcum powder. Colored with chalk. Did you touch, breathe or ingest anything else in that lab? Were you inoculated with anything?"

"No, sir."

"You're positive?"

"Yes, sir."

He asked me more questions until he was satisfied I hadn't ingested or inhaled anything but colored chalk. Then he twirled me around, looked at every inch of my body and tested me for contamination.

I remembered the colored powdery sands on Brandy's window sill. It appeared Dr. Bigsby had learned a lot from Brandy.

Sam gave me a stern look. "You are absolutely sure you did not touch or ingest anything in that lab?"

"Yes."

"I think the hospital should check you out," he said.

"I'm perfectly fine. I just want to go home."

"That's up to our EMS lieutenant," the fireman said. "We need to check the rest of you."

When they finished testing us, the Hazmat fireman waved to a man standing by the vehicles. "All clear. No contamination."

The EMS lieutenant, who was apparently the medic in charge, answered, "Okay. We're ready for transport."

"I need to go talk to him," Sam said. "If we're clear, we should be able to leave in my car."

He strode toward the medic. After what seemed like an endless conversation, he came back. "Okay. The lieutenant called his medical director. We sign releases and we're free to leave."

We walked to the vehicles and scribbled our names. I looked at

Sam. "Can I go home now?"

"I'll take her," Sam said. "You can release her to my custody."

The EMS lieutenant gave Sam another paper to sign.

"All right then," District Chief Lansing said. "She's yours, Detective." I liked the sound of that.

Chief Lansing radioed to the team inside the lab. "Once the victim inside is decontaminated, bring her to the cold zone and seal the lab and the building."

When they hauled Dr. Bigsby out on a stretcher, I heard her moan. They carried her to the EMS van.

"What happens next?" I asked Sam.

"It looks like she's been cleared for cold zone transport by EMS. They'll wire ahead to the hospital and have them prepare an isolation unit, just to be safe. Then hospital doctors will treat her injuries." He held open the door for me, and I got into his car. He swung into the driver's seat and pulled away from the curb.

"It's really sad," I said. "With her intellect and drive, she could have been a successful and elegant woman. She was so obsessed with being what she thought Dr. Carmody wanted her to be, his scientific comrade, that she lost perspective about her full potential."

Sam looked over at me. Had I made the same mistake with him? I'd made a ton of mistakes, and it was too late to correct them.

"When that Brandy chick sunk her claws into Carmody, that's when Dr. Bigsby must have snapped."

Sam didn't seem interested in Dr. Bigsby's psychology. I think he was more concerned with mine.

I waited as long as I could for him to talk. When he didn't, I decided to tell him what else I'd learned, like details of our lunch conversation with Brandy and her boyfriends. "I think those three, plus Bigsby—if she hasn't totally schizzed out—will know exactly what Carmody and Eric Lager were doing in the lab."

"Our guys followed those scientists from the cafeteria and interviewed them this morning. We thought Carmody and Eric Lager might be secretly collaborating, since they both turned up dead. But the postdocs told us they were very familiar with every experiment in the lab. They said so many researchers worked on similar projects in conjunction with the Human Genome Project, and there was so much collaboration between labs, it was doubtful Carmody and Lager could have been going in a direction nobody else knew about. They said professors like Carmody direct the research but almost never touch the lab. The standard joke is that a professor who walks into the lab is liable to break something. The research group of graduate students, postdocs, and a few undergrads actually do the lab work. Any hands-on work by professors is only to teach undergrads. We'll check out the postdocs' story, of course."

"The locked drawer in the lab behind where I stood could have Carmody's research notes in it and maybe the list of his scientific colleagues."

"We'll check it."

"So," I said, "all Hortense Bigsby's talk about Carmody and Lager making a breakthrough was just to prop up Carmody's legacy and her own fantasies?"

"Looks that way."

"What was all that stuff in the incubator she used to threaten me?"

"Probably a bunch of worthless concoctions. Hazmat will test it. Scientists have told us NIH has strict protocols, which must be approved long ahead of time, for taking samples from human subjects. If your cells and genes are in that incubator, Bigsby's actions would be highly illegal."

"Probably not as illegal as murder though."

"Right. I think I'll take you home, Aggie. We can get your car later."

"Did the medical examiner find out what killed Eric Lager?"

"Yes. Cyanide in his nasal spray. Bigsby was on a roll with spray bottles. She apparently dissolved sodium cyanide salt into saline spray and substituted it for Lager's nasal spray."

"Since so many people suffer from allergies, I guess she found the method pretty useful. And she could get whatever she wanted from the lab's chemical stockroom."

"Yes. There will be prints on gloves she used to mix the chemicals and on Eric Lager's spray bottle. They found something else in the stockroom: a flashlight with Lager's fingerprints on one end and blood traces on the other end, like he'd hit somebody with it. Did he hit you on the head the night you told me you fell?"

I nodded. "I wasn't sure who did it. Now I know it was him." I sighed. "What a semester. I learned a lot about genetics, and a ton about professional jealousy, but not nearly enough to stay young."

He didn't say another word all the way to my house.

Sixty

Sam stood silently and watched me unlock my front door. The minute we stepped inside, he took my arm and led me to the sofa. I plopped down and waited for whatever was coming.

He clicked on my pen recorder to make sure it worked, listened a few minutes and went to the phone. He called my attorney and told him Bigsby had killed both men, and that he had evidence to prove my innocence.

He hung up. "Matheson says if our evidence holds, he'll contact the court to drop charges against you. He said Meredith might have paid him enough to help your jail friends."

I let out a sigh. "I'll repay Meredith."

"There's something else I want to discuss with you, Aggie." He sat by me on the couch.

I dreaded hearing what he was going to say. I knew I'd made everything difficult for myself and for Sam with my lies and omissions. But I'd had all the trauma I could take for one day.

He took my hands. "I think you're beautiful, Aggie, exactly as you are. Well, maybe after a bath." He grinned at me. "And you're young. You always will be, because you're eager and interested and empathetic and too damn curious for your own good."

I frowned. I wasn't sure where this was going.

"Did you notice that Phillip Delay looks a little like Dr. Carmody?" I asked. "I wondered if he might be related, might even be his son."

"We noticed and checked him out. He's not related to

Carmody. But you are amazingly perceptive about people, Aggie—about their motives and why they might commit crimes. You've proven to me you can be a great investigator and help on a case."

My heart skipped. "Did I tell you about the colored powders Brandy has on her windowsill? One of them looks just like that powder Dr. Bigsby made me sniff."

"We'll analyze all the powders. Aggie, you don't need to investigate crimes to impress me. I can't always be afraid for you. I can't do my job and wonder if I'm going to lose you because of it. You even lied to me about being hit on the head. I have enough pressure without that."

I hung my head. He was right.

"I don't want any more secrets between us."

Now he was really making me nervous.

He reached in his pocket and held up a plastic bracelet. A baby's bracelet...my baby's bracelet!

I shrunk back from him. "Where did you get that?"

"Detective Sheffield found it on the lawn outside the lab the night you were arrested. He gave it to me later at the station. It didn't mean a whole lot to me at first. I thought it was some trinket. I didn't even look at it. I almost threw it away. For some reason, I stuck it in a drawer.

"I always wondered, when we lived in Chicago, and you decided to work at the branch bank for six months, why you transferred there. I wondered whether it had to do with Lester. Not long after you stopped telling Katy and me about him, you left. I assumed you stopped dating him and wondered if you left because of him."

I covered my face with my hands and hung my head. He was never supposed to know. Katy had promised she'd never tell him.

"I pulled out the bracelet again. I realized you might have lost it. When I saw it was a baby's hospital bracelet, I read the names on it. Yours and Lee's."

I started sobbing. I thought I was going to be ill. My whole relationship with him and Lee had been a lie. He and Katy had raised her as their own with me, Lee's biological mother, right under their nose. I wanted him to leave me alone and go away so I'd never have to see him again. But he wouldn't stop talking.

"When Katy and I talked about naming our baby girl, she brought up the name Lee. It wasn't a family name, but she seemed to like it a lot, and it did go with other names. So we named our daughter Susan Lee Vanderhoven. But we called her Lee. She was your daughter too, wasn't she, Aggie?"

By this time, I was bawling. My stomach hurt, and I couldn't look at him. I put my face in my hands. He sat and let me cry until I couldn't cry anymore. When I heard him walk away, my heart dropped in my chest like a stone.

But he came back with a box of Kleenex and touched my shoulder. I took it, blew my nose and wiped my eyes. When I was able to look at his face, his eyes were sad but not hateful.

He sat down. "Now," he said. "You need to know something else. I don't hate you. I could never hate you. I was angry at first that you didn't tell me, but the more I thought about it, I understood why you didn't. Why you couldn't. I realized you gave Lee to us because you loved us. You thought we'd be the best parents for her. And you couldn't keep her yourself."

I started crying again, nodding and nodding.

"I understand. I've always felt a bond between us, even when I loved Katy. The bond is Lee. And, Aggie..."

"Yes?"

"I love you. I think I've loved you for a long time." He pulled me into his arms.

I clung to him. "I've loved you since we were in Chicago," I said. "But you loved Katy, and I couldn't interfere with that. I dated Lester because I wanted what you and Katy had. I was so naive and foolish. Lester was nothing like you. Can you ever forgive me?"

"About Lee? I already have." He pulled back from me and smiled. "I'm still thinking about your other infractions."

I couldn't help but smile. With red eyes and purplish-red powder streaking down my face, I must have looked like a goofy clown. He leaned forward and kissed my cheek.

I'd been transported to another place. Another life. And I didn't feel one bit older. Maybe I never would. Maybe that's what love did. I pulled back and looked at him.

"Now what do we do?"

He leaned back against the couch, took a deep breath and closed his eyes momentarily before he looked back at me. "I think we need to meet each other again for the first time. Without pressure. Without crime. And without secrets."

I nodded. "Where could that possibly be?"

"I don't know. Maybe a trip. A cruise. A vacation at some resort."

I recalled our dude ranch vacation. It had been pretty traumatic. But I wasn't about to interrupt when he was making plans for us. I silently swore I would not be so meddlesome. And I was determined to be truthful.

"There could be other people there," he said. "Maybe Meredith would want to come. We'd have time to get to know each other in a different light. Without emotions from the past always weighing us down."

"And without any secrets between us."

"Exactly."

I started smiling. I couldn't stop. I was grinning like an idiot.

"Why don't you start thinking about where we might go? I'll call you later," he said.

I smiled him to the door, smiled when he got into the car and smiled him down the street until I couldn't see him anymore.

I didn't even wash my face. I plopped on my bedspread, face up, and flapped my arms and legs like a fresh snow angel.

I was Aggie Mundeen. And I was never going to grow old.

Afterword

Cynthia Kenyon: Future – Aging – Facing the Challenge

Thanks to the pioneering studies by Kenyon there is now a strong reason to think that genetic or drug-induced extension of lifespan could delay the onset of diseases of old age. This concept has revolutionary implications.

Cynthia Kenyon became involved in investigating the aging process in the early 1990s. By comparing *C. elegans* worms with normal (short) lifespan and long-lived *C. elegans* mutants, Kenyon discovered that mutations that reduced the activity of the daf-2 gene doubled the lifespan of the worms which remained youthful and active much longer than their wild-type, normal counterparts. These observations suggested that daf-2 mutations altered the rate of aging demonstrating that a single specific gene could have a truly profound effect on aging.

Kenyon also discovered the daf-16 gene being the one that could keep an animal young. The daf-2 and daf-16 genes affect lifespan by influencing the level of the body's antioxidants, the integrity of its immune system, its ability to repair its proteins, and many other beneficial processes. Another important finding of Kenyon was that the daf-16 gene is influenced by signals from the environment and also by signals from the reproductive system. This finding was used to extend the lifespan of worms by six fold.

Other investigators showed that daf-2-like genes control the lifespan of fruit flies, mice and possibly also humans. When these genes are changed, aging is slowed and lifespan is extended.

In summarizing her own achievements and those of her research team, Cynthia Kenyon wrote: "To me it seems possible that a fountain of youth, made of molecules and not simply dreams, will someday be a reality."

2015 Update from Dr. Cynthia Kenyon

I hope readers don't think that I think that we will ever be immortal. I'm hoping that using this information, humans will one day be able to remain youthful and free of age-related disease for a longer time (have a longer "health span"). We don't know if nudging these molecules will slow aging in humans, although there are hints that it might.

-Cynthia Kenyon
July 2, 2015

Among Cynthia Kenyon's honors are a member of the National Academy of Sciences; American Academy of Arts & Science; Honorary Doctorate, University of Paris; King Faisal International Prize for Medicine, La Foundation IPSEN Prize; and the AARP Inspire Award.

Nancy G. West

While writing her award-winning suspense novel, *Nine Days to Evil*, a funny thing happened. Supporting character Aggie Mundeen demanded that Nancy write about her. Aggie's first caper, *Fit to Be Dead*, was Lefty Award Finalist for Best Humorous Mystery. *Dang Near Dead* was named a "Must Read" by *Southern Writers Magazine*. In *Smart, But Dead*, Aggie learns genetic secrets of staying young and critical lessons about love and about staying alive.

In Case You Missed the 1st Book in the Series

FIT TO BE DEAD

Nancy G. West

An Aggie Mundeen Mystery (#1)

Aggie Mundeen, single and pushing forty, fears nothing but middle age. When she moves from Chicago to San Antonio, she decides she better shape up before anybody discovers she writes the column, "Stay Young with Aggie." She takes Aspects of Aging at University of the Holy Trinity and plunges into exercise at Fit and Firm.

Rusty at flirting and mechanically inept, she irritates a slew of male exercisers, then stumbles into murder. She'd like to impress the attractive detective with her sleuthing skills. But when the killer comes after her, the health club evacuates semi-clad patrons, and the detective has to stall his investigation to save Aggie's derriere.

Available at booksellers nationwide and online

Visit www.henerypress.com for details

In Case You Missed the 2nd Book in the Series

DANG NEAR DEAD

Nancy G. West

An Aggie Mundeen Mystery (#2)

Aggie takes a vacation with Sam and Meredith at a Texas Hill Country dude ranch with plans to advise her column readers how to stay young and fresh in summer. Except for wranglers, dudes, heat, snakes and poison ivy, what could go wrong?

When an expert rider is thrown from a horse and lies in a coma, Aggie is convinced somebody caused the fall. Despite Sam's warnings, Aggie is determined to expose the assailant. She concocts ingenious sleuthing methods that strain their dicey relationship as she probes secrets of the ranch and its inhabitants. After she scatters a hornet's nest of cowboys, she discovers more than one hombre in the bunch would like to slit her throat.

Available at booksellers nationwide and online

Visit www.henerypress.com for details

Henery Press Mystery Books

And finally, before you go...
Here are a few other mysteries
you might enjoy:

PORTRAIT OF A DEAD GUY

Larissa Reinhart

A Cherry Tucker Mystery (#1)

In Halo, Georgia, folks know Cherry Tucker as big in mouth, small in stature, and able to sketch a portrait faster than buck-shot rips from a ten gauge -- but commissions are scarce. So when the well-heeled Branson family wants to memorialize their murdered son in a coffin portrait, Cherry scrambles to win their patronage from her small town rival.

As the clock ticks toward the deadline, Cherry faces more trouble than just a controversial subject. Between ex-boyfriends, her flaky family, an illegal gambling ring, and outwitting a killer on a spree, Cherry finds herself painted into a corner she'll be lucky to survive.

Available at booksellers nationwide and online

Visit www.henerypress.com for details

FRONT PAGE FATALITY

LynDee Walker

A Headlines in High Heels Mystery (#1)

Crime reporter Nichelle Clarke's days can flip from macabre to comical with a beep of her police scanner. Then an ordinary accident story turns extraordinary when evidence goes missing, a prosecutor vanishes, and a sexy Mafia boss shows up with the headline tip of a lifetime.

As Nichelle gets closer to the truth, her story gets more dangerous. Armed with a notebook, a hunch, and her favorite stilettos, Nichelle races to splash these shady dealings across the front page before this deadline becomes her last.

Available at booksellers nationwide and online

Visit www.henerypress.com for details

CROPPED TO DEATH

Christina Freeburn

A Faith Hunter Scrap This Mystery (#1)

Former US Army JAG specialist, Faith Hunter, returns to her West Virginia home to work in her grandmothers' scrapbooking store determined to lead an unassuming life after her adventure abroad turned disaster. But her quiet life unravels when her friend is charged with murder – and Faith inadvertently supplied the evidence. So Faith decides to cut through the scrap and piece together what really happened.

With a sexy prosecutor, a determined homicide detective, a handful of sticky suspects and a crop contest gone bad, Faith quickly realizes if she's not careful, she'll be the next one cropped.

Available at booksellers nationwide and online

Visit www.henerypress.com for details

MURDER ON A SILVER PLATTER

Shawn Reilly Simmons

A Red Carpet Catering Mystery (#1)

Penelope Sutherland and her Red Carpet Catering company just got their big break as the on-set caterer for an upcoming blockbuster. But when she discovers a dead body outside her house, Penelope finds herself in hot water. Things start to boil over when serious accidents threaten the lives of the cast and crew. And when the film's star, who happens to be Penelope's best friend, is poisoned, the entire production is nearly shut down.

Threats and accusations send Penelope out of the frying pan and into the fire as she struggles to keep her company afloat. Before Penelope can dish up dessert, she must find the killer or she'll be the one served up on a silver platter.

Available at booksellers nationwide and online

Visit www.henerypress.com for details

CPSIA information can be obtained
at www.ICGtesting.com
Printed in the USA
LVOW04s1512040216

473701LV00020B/853/P